Ignorance

Milan Kundera

Ignorance

*Translated from the French by
Linda Asher*

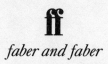

faber and faber

First published in 2002 by HarperCollins US
First published in Great Britain in 2002
by Faber and Faber Limited
3, Queen Square, London WC1N 3AU

Printed in England by Clays Ltd, St Ives plc

A CIP record for this book
is available from the British Library

ISBN 0–571–21550–5

2 4 6 8 10 9 7 5 3 1

Ignorance

1

"What are you still doing here?" Her tone wasn't harsh, but it wasn't kindly, either; Sylvie was indignant.

"Where should I be?" Irena asked.

"Home!"

"You mean this isn't my home anymore?"

Of course she wasn't trying to drive Irena out of France or implying that she was an undesirable alien: "You know what I mean!"

"Yes, I do know, but aren't you forgetting that I've got my work here? My apartment? My children?"

"Look, I know Gustaf. He'll do anything to help you get back to your own country. And your daughters, let's not kid ourselves! They've already got their own lives. Good Lord, Irena, it's so fascinating, what's going on in your country! In a situation like that, things always work out."

"But Sylvie! It's not just a matter of practical things, the job, the apartment. I've been living here for twenty years now. My life is here!"

"Your people have a revolution going on!"

Sylvie spoke in a tone that brooked no objection. Then she said no more. By her silence she meant to tell Irena that you don't desert when great events are happening.

"But if I go back to my country, we won't see each other anymore," said Irena, to put her friend in an uncomfortable position.

That emotional demagognery miscarried. Sylvie's voice warmed: "Darling, I'll come see you! I promise, I promise!"

They were seated across from each other, over two empty coffee cups. Irena saw tears of emotion in Sylvie's eyes as her friend bent toward her and gripped her hand: "It will be your great return." And again: "Your great return."

Repeated, the words took on such power that, deep inside her, Irena saw them written out with capital initials: Great Return. She dropped her resistance: she was captivated by images suddenly welling up from books read long ago, from films, from her own memory, and maybe from her ancestral memory: the lost son home again with his aged mother; the man returning to his beloved from whom cruel destiny had torn him away; the family homestead we all carry about within us;

4

the rediscovered trail still marked by the forgotten footprints of childhood; Odysseus sighting his island after years of wandering; the return, the return, the great magic of the return.

2

The Greek word for "return" is *nostos. Algos* means "suffering." So nostalgia is the suffering caused by an unappeased yearning to return. To express that fundamental notion most Europeans can utilize a word derived from the Greek (*nostalgia, nostalgie*) as well as other words with roots in their national languages: *añoranza*, say the Spaniards; *saudade*, say the Portuguese. In each language these words have a different semantic nuance. Often they mean only the sadness caused by the impossibility of returning to one's country: a longing for country, for home. What in English is called "homesickness." Or in German: *Heimweh*. In Dutch: *heimwee*. But this reduces that great notion to just its spatial element. One of the oldest European languages, Icelandic (like English) makes a distinction between two terms: *söknuður*: nostalgia in its general sense; and *heimþrá*: longing for the homeland. Czechs have the Greek-derived *nostalgie* as well as their own noun, *stesk*, and their own verb; the most moving Czech expression of love: *styska se mi po tobe* ("I yearn for you," "I'm nostalgic for you"; "I cannot bear the pain of your absence"). In Spanish *añoranza* comes from the verb *añorar* (to feel nostalgia), which comes from the Catalan *enyorar*, itself derived from the Latin word *ignorare* (to be unaware of, not know, not experience; to lack or miss). In that etymological light nostalgia seems something like the pain of ignorance, of not knowing. You are far away, and I don't know what has become of you. My country is far away, and I don't know what is happening there. Certain languages have problems with nostalgia: the French can only express it by the noun from the Greek root, and have no verb for it; they can say *Je m'ennuie de toi* (I miss you), but the word *s'ennuyer* is weak, cold—anyhow too light for so grave a feeling. The Germans rarely use the Greek-derived term *Nostalgie*, and tend to say *Sehnsucht* in speaking of the desire for an absent thing. But

Sehnsucht can refer both to something that has existed and to something that has never existed (a new adventure), and therefore it does not necessarily imply the *nostos* idea; to include in *Sehnsucht* the obsession with returning would require adding a complementary phrase: *Sehnsucht nach der Vergangenheit, nach der verlorenen Kindheit, nach der ersten Liebe* (longing for the past, for lost childhood, for a first love).

The dawn of ancient Greek culture brought the birth of the *Odyssey*, the founding epic of nostalgia. Let us emphasize: Odysseus, the greatest adventurer of all time, is also the greatest nostalgic. He went off (not very happily) to the Trojan War and stayed for ten years. Then he tried to return to his native Ithaca, but the gods' intrigues prolonged his journey, first by three years jammed with the most uncanny happenings, then by seven more years that he spent as hostage and lover with Calypso, who in her passion for him would not let him leave her island.

In Book Five of the *Odyssey*, Odysseus tells Calypso: "As wise as she is, I know that Penelope cannot compare to you in stature or in beauty. . . . And yet the only wish I wish each day is to be back there, to see in my own house the day of my return!" And Homer goes on: "As Odysseus spoke, the sun sank; the dusk came: and beneath the vault deep within the cavern, they withdrew to lie and love in each other's arms."

A far cry from the life of the poor émigré that Irena had been for a long while now. Odysseus lived a real *dolce vita* there in Calypso's land, a life of ease, a life of delights. And yet, between the *dolce vita* in a foreign place and the risky return to his home, he chose the return. Rather than ardent exploration of the unknown (adventure), he chose the apotheosis of the known (return). Rather than the infinite (for adventure never intends to finish), he chose the finite (for the return is a reconciliation with the finitude of life).

Without waking him, the Phaeacian seamen laid Odysseus, still wrapped in his bedding, near an olive tree on Ithaca's shore, and then departed. Such was his journey's end. He slept on, exhausted. When he awoke, he could not tell where he was. Then Athena wiped the mist from his eyes and it was rapture; the rapture of the Great Return; the ecstasy of the known; the music that sets the air vibrating between earth and heaven: he saw the harbor he had known since childhood, the mountain overlooking it, and he fondled the old olive tree to confirm that it was still the same as it had been twenty years earlier.

In 1950, when Arnold Schoenberg had been in the United States for seventeen years, a journalist asked him a few treacherously innocent questions: Is it true that emigration causes artists to lose their creativity? That their inspiration withers when it no longer has the roots of their native land to nourish it?

Imagine! Five years after the Holocaust! And an American journalist won't forgive Schoenberg his lack of attachment to that chunk of earth where, before his very eyes, the horror of horrors started! But it's a lost cause. Homer glorified nostalgia with a laurel wreath and thereby laid out a moral hierarchy of emotions. Penelope stands at its summit, very high above Calypso.

Calypso, ah, Calypso! I often think about her. She loved Odysseus. They lived together for seven years. We do not know how long Odysseus shared Penelope's bed, but certainly not so long as that. And yet we extol Penelope's pain and sneer at Calypso's tears.

9

3

Like blows from an ax, important dates cut deep gashes into Europe's twentieth century. The First World War, in 1914; the second; then the third—the longest one, known as "the Cold"—ending in 1989 with the disappearance of Communism. Beyond these important dates that apply to Europe as a whole, dates of secondary importance define the fates of particular nations: the year 1936, with the civil war in Spain; 1956, with Russia's invasion of Hungary; 1948, when the Yugoslavs rose up against Stalin; and 1991, when they set about slaughtering one another. The Scandinavians, the Dutch, the English are privileged to have had no important dates since 1945, which has allowed them to live a delightfully null half century.

The history of the Czechs in the twentieth century is graced with a remarkable mathematical beauty owing to the triple repetition of the number twenty. In 1918, after several centuries, they achieved their independence, and in 1938 they lost it.

In 1948 the Communist revolution, imported from Moscow, inaugurated the country's second twenty-year span; that one ended in 1968 when, enraged by the country's insolent self-emancipation, the Russians invaded with half a million soldiers.

The occupier took over in full force in the autumn of 1969 and then, to everyone's surprise, took off in autumn 1989—quietly, politely, as did all the Communist regimes in Europe at that time: and that was the third twenty-year span.

Our century is the only one in which historic dates have taken such a voracious grip on every single person's life. Irena's existence in France cannot be understood without first analyzing the dates. In the fifties and sixties, émigrés from the Communist countries were not much liked there; the French considered the sole true evil to be fascism: Hitler, Mussolini, Franco, the dictators in Latin America. Only gradually, late in the sixties and into the seventies, did they come to see Communism, too, as an evil, although one of a lesser degree—say, evil number two. That was when, in 1969, Irena and her husband emigrated to France. They soon realized that compared with the number one evil, the catastrophe that had befallen their country was not bloody enough to impress their new friends. To make their position clear, they took to saying something like this:

"Horrible as it is, a fascist dictatorship will disappear when its dictator does, and therefore people can keep up hope. But Communism, which is sustained by the enormous Russian civilization, is an endless tunnel for a Poland, a Hungary (not even to mention an Estonia!). Dictators are perishable, Russia is eternal. The misery of the countries we come from lies in the utter absence of hope."

This was the accurate expression of their thinking, and to illustrate it, Irena would quote a stanza from Jan Skacel, a Czech poet of the period: he describes the sadness surrounding him; he wants to take that sadness in his hands, carry it far off somewhere and build himself a house out of it, he wants to lock himself inside that house for three hundred years and for three hundred years not open the door, not open the door to anyone!

Three hundred years? Skacel wrote those lines in the 1970s and he died in 1989, in autumn, just a few days before those three hundred years of sadness he saw stretching ahead crumbled in just a few days: people filled the Prague streets, and the key rings jangling in their lifted hands rang in the coming of a new age.

Did Skacel have it wrong when he spoke of three hundred years? Of course he did. All predictions are wrong, that's one of the few certainties granted to mankind. But though predictions may be wrong, they are right about the people who voice them, not about their future but about their experience of the present moment. During what I call their first twenty-year span (between 1918 and 1938), the Czechs believed that their republic had all infinity ahead of it. They had it wrong, but precisely because they were wrong, they lived those years in a state of joy that led their arts to flourish as never before.

After the Russian invasion, since they had no inkling of Communism's eventual end, they again believed they were inhabiting an infinity, and it was not the pain of their current life but the vacuity of the future that sucked dry their energies, stifled their courage, and made that third twenty-year span so craven, so wretched.

In 1921, convinced that with his twelve-tone system he had opened far-reaching prospects to musical history, Arnold Schoenberg declared that thanks to him, predominance (he didn't say "glory," he said *Vorherrschaft*, "predominance") was guaranteed to German music (he, a Viennese, didn't say "Austrian," he said "German") for the next hundred years (I quote him exactly, he spoke of "a hundred years"). A dozen years after that prophecy, in 1933, he was forced, as a Jew, to leave Germany (the very Germany for which he sought to guarantee *Vorherrschaft*), as was all music based on his twelve-tone system (which was condemned as incomprehensible, elitist, cosmopolitan, and hostile to the German spirit).

Schoenberg's prognosis, however mistaken, is nonetheless indispensable for anyone seeking to understand the meaning of his work, which he considered not destructive, hermetic, cosmopolitan, individualistic, difficult, or abstract but, rather, deeply rooted in "German soil" (yes, he spoke of "German soil"); Schoenberg believed he was writing not a fascinating epilogue to the history of Europe's great music (which is how I tend to see his work) but the prologue to a glorious future stretching farther than the eye could see.

4

From the very first weeks after emigrating, Irena began to have strange dreams: she is in an airplane that switches direction and lands at an unknown airport; uniformed men with guns are waiting for her at the foot of the gangway; in a cold sweat, she recognizes the Czech police. Another time she is strolling in a small French city when she sees an odd group of women, each holding a beer mug, run toward her, call to her in Czech, laugh with fake cordiality, and in terror Irena realizes that she is in Prague. She cries out, she wakes up.

Martin, her husband, was having the same dreams. Every morning they would talk about the horror of that return to their native land. Then, in the course of a conversation with a Polish friend, an émigré herself, Irena realized that all émigrés had those dreams, every one, without exception; at first she was moved by that nighttime fraternity of people unknown to one another, then somewhat irritated: how could the very private experience of a dream be a collective event? what was unique about her soul, then? But that's

15

enough of questions that have no answers! One thing was certain: on any given night, thousands of émigrés were all dreaming the same dream in numberless variants. The emigration-dream: one of the strangest phenomena of the second half of the twentieth century.

These dream-nightmares seemed to her all the more mysterious in that she was afflicted simultaneously with an uncontrollable nostalgia and another, completely opposite, experience: landscapes from her country kept appearing to her by day. No, this was not daydreaming, lengthy and conscious, willed; it was something else entirely: visions of landscapes would blink on in her head unexpectedly, abruptly, swiftly, and go out instantly. She would be talking to her boss and all at once, like a flash of lightning, she'd see a path through a field. She would be jostled on the Métro and suddenly, a narrow lane in some leafy Prague neighborhood would rise up before her for a split second. All day long these fleeting images would visit her to assuage the longing for her lost Bohemia.

The same moviemaker of the subconscious who, by day, was sending her bits of the home

landscape as images of happiness, by night would
set up terrifying returns to that same land. The
day was lit with the beauty of the land forsaken,
the night by the horror of returning to it. The day
would show her the paradise she had lost; the
night, the hell she had fled.

5

Loyal to the tradition of the French Revolution,
the Communist countries hurled anathema at
emigration, deemed to be the most odious trea-
son. Everyone who stayed abroad was convicted
in absentia in their home country, and their compatriots did not dare have any contact with them.
Still, as time passed, the severity of the anathema
weakened, and a few years before 1989, Irena's
mother, an inoffensive pensioner recently widowed, was granted an exit visa for a weeklong trip
to Italy through the government travel agency;
the following year she decided to spend five days
in Paris and secretly see her daughter. Touched,
and full of pity for a mother she imagined had

grown elderly, Irena booked her a hotel room and sacrificed some vacation time so she could be with her the whole while.

"You don't look too bad," the mother said when they first met. Then, laughing, she added: "Neither do I, actually. When the border policeman looked at my passport, he said: 'This is a false passport, Madame! This is not your date of birth!'" Instantly Irena recognized her mother as the person she had always known, and she had the sense that nothing had changed in those nearly twenty years. The pity she'd felt for an elderly mother evaporated. Daughter and mother faced off like two beings outside time, like two timeless essences.

But wasn't it awful of the daughter not to be delighted at the presence of her mother who, after seventeen years, had come to see her? Irena mustered all her rationality, all her moral discipline, to behave like a devoted daughter. She took her mother to dinner at the restaurant up in the Eiffel Tower; she took her on a tour boat to show her Paris from the Seine; and because the mother wanted to see art, she took her to the Musée Picasso. In the second gallery the mother stopped short: "I've got a friend who's a painter. She gave me two pictures as a gift. You can't imagine how beautiful they are!" In the third gallery she declared she wanted to see the Impressionists: "There's a permanent exhibition at the Jeu de Paume." "That's gone now," Irena said. "The Impressionists aren't at the Jeu de Paume anymore." "No, no," said the mother. "They are, they're at the Jeu de Paume. I know they are, and I'm not leaving Paris without seeing van Gogh!" Irena took her instead to the Musée Rodin. Standing in front of one of his statues, the mother sighed dreamily: "In Florence I saw Michelangelo's *David*! I was just speechless!" "Listen," Irena exploded. "You're here in Paris with me, and I'm showing you Rodin. Rodin! You hear? Rodin! You've never seen him, so why are you thinking about Michelangelo when you're right in front of Rodin?"

The question was fair: why, when she is reunited with her daughter after years, does the mother take no interest in what the younger woman is showing her and telling her? Why does Michelangelo, whom she saw with a group of Czech tourists, captivate her more than Rodin?

19

And why, through all these five days, does she not ask her daughter a single question? Not one question about her life, and none about France either—about its cuisine, its literature, its cheeses, its wines, its politics, its theaters, its films, its cars, its pianists, its cellists, its athletes?

Instead she talks constantly about goings-on in Prague, about Irena's half-brother (by her second husband, the one who just died), about other people, some Irena remembers and some she's never heard of. A couple of times she's tried to inject a remark about her life in France, but her words never penetrate the chinkless barrier of the mother's discourse.

That's how it had been ever since she was a child: the mother fussed over her son as if he were a little girl, but was manfully Spartan toward her daughter. Do I mean that she did not love her daughter? Perhaps because of Irena's father, her first husband, whom she had despised? We won't indulge in that sort of cheap psychologizing. Her behavior was very well intentioned: overflowing with energy and health herself, she worried over her daughter's low vitality; her rough style was meant to rid the daughter of her hypersensitivity, rather like an athletic father who throws his fear-

20

ful child into the swimming pool in the belief that this is the best way to teach him to swim.

And yet she was fully aware that her mere presence flattened her daughter, and I won't deny that she took a secret pleasure in her own physical superiority. So? What was she supposed to do? Vanish into thin air in the name of maternal love? She was growing inexorably older, and the sense of her strength as reflected in Irena's reaction had a rejuvenating effect on her. When she saw her daughter cowed and diminished at her side, she would prolong the occasions of her demolishing supremacy as long as possible. With sadistic zest, she would pretend to take Irena's fragility for indifference, laziness, indolence, and scolded her for it.

Irena had always felt less pretty and less intelligent in her mother's presence. How often had she run to the mirror for reassurance that she wasn't ugly, didn't look like an idiot . . . ? Oh, all that was so far away, almost forgotten. But during her mother's five-day stay in Paris, that feeling of inferiority, of weakness, of dependency came over her again.

6

The night before her mother left, Irena introduced her to her companion, Gustaf, a Swede. The three of them had dinner in a restaurant, and the mother, who spoke not a word of French, managed valiantly with English. Gustaf was delighted: with his mistress, Irena, he spoke only French, and he was tired of that language, which he considered pretentious and not very practical. That evening Irena did not talk much: she looked on in surprise as her mother displayed an unexpected capacity for interest in another person; with just her thirty badly pronounced English words she overwhelmed Gustaf with questions about his life, his business, his views, and she impressed him.

The next day her mother left. Back from the airport, and back to peace in her top-floor apartment, Irena went to the window to savor the freedom of solitude. She gazed for a long while out at the rooftops, the array of chimneys with all their different fantastical shapes—the Parisian flora that had long ago supplanted the green of Czech gardens—and she realized how happy she was in this city. She had always taken it as a given that emigrating was a misfortune. But, now she wonders, wasn't it instead an illusion of misfortune, an illusion suggested by the way people perceive an émigré? Wasn't she interpreting her own life according to the operating instructions other people had handed her? And she thought that even though it had been imposed from the outside and against her will, her emigration was perhaps, without her knowing it, the best outcome for her life. The implacable forces of history that had attacked her freedom had set her free.

So she was a little disconcerted a few weeks later when Gustaf proudly announced some good news: he had proposed that his firm open a Prague office. Since the Communist country had limited commercial appeal, the office would be a modest one; still, he would have occasion to spend time there now and then.

"I'm thrilled to have a connection with your city," he said.

Rather than delight, she felt some sort of vague threat.

"My city? Prague isn't my city anymore," she answered.

23

"What?" He bristled.

She had never disguised her views from him, so it was certainly possible for him to know her well, and yet he was seeing her exactly the way everyone else saw her: *a young woman in pain, banished from her country.* He himself comes from a Swedish town he wholeheartedly detests, and in which he refuses to set foot. But in his case it's taken for granted. Because everyone applauds him as *a nice, very cosmopolitan Scandinavian who's already forgotten all about the place he comes from.* Both of them are pigeonholed, labeled, and they will be judged by how true they are to their labels (of course, that and that alone is what's emphatically called "being true to oneself").

"What are you saying!" he protested. "Then what is your city?"

"Paris! This is where I met you, where I live with you."

As if he hadn't heard her, he stroked her hand: "Accept this as my gift to you. You can't go there. So I'll be your link to your lost country. I'm happy to do it!"

She did not doubt his goodness; she thanked

him; nonetheless she added, her tone even: "But please do understand that I don't need you to be my link with anything at all. I'm happy with you, cut off from everything and everyone."

He responded just as soberly: "I understand what you're saying. And don't worry that I expect to involve myself in your old life there. The only one I'll see of the people you used to know will be your mother."

What could she say? That her mother is exactly the person she doesn't want him spending time with? How could she tell him that—this man who remembers his own dead mother with such love?

"I admire your mother. What vitality!"

Irena has no doubt of that. Everyone admires her mother for her vitality. How can she explain to Gustaf that within the magic circle of maternal energy, Irena has never managed to rule over her own life? How can she explain that the constant proximity of the mother would throw her back, into her weaknesses, her immaturity? Oh, this insane idea of Gustaf's, wanting to connect with Prague!

Only when she was alone, back in the house, did she calm down, telling herself: "The police barrier between the Communist countries and the West is pretty solid, thank God. I don't have to worry that Gustaf's contacts with Prague could be any threat to me."

What? What was that she just said to herself? "The police barrier is pretty solid, thank God?" Did she really say, "Thank God?" Did she—an émigré everyone pities for losing her homeland—did she actually say, "Thank God?"

7

Gustaf had come to know Martin by chance, over a business negotiation. He met Irena much later, when she was already widowed. They liked each other, but they were shy. Whereupon the husband hurried in from the beyond to help them along by being a ready subject for conversation. When Gustaf learned from Irena that Martin had been born the same year he was, he heard the collapse of the wall that separated him from this much-younger woman, and he felt a grateful affection for the dead man whose age encouraged him to court the man's beautiful wife.

26

Gustaf worshipped his deceased mother; he tolerated (without pleasure) two grown daughters; he was fleeing his wife. He would very much have liked to divorce if it could be done amicably. Since that was impossible, he did his best to stay away from Sweden. Like him, Irena had two daughters, who were also on the brink of living on their own. For the elder one Gustaf bought a studio apartment, and he arranged to send the younger one to a boarding school in England, so that Irena, living alone, could take him in.

She was dazzled by his goodness, which everyone saw as the main trait, the most striking, almost unbelievable trait of his character. He charmed women by it; they understood only too late that the goodness was less a weapon of seduction than a weapon of defense. His mother's darling boy, he was incapable of living on his own without women's caretaking. But he tolerated all the less well their demands, their arguments, their tears, and even their too-present, too-expansive bodies. To keep them around and at the same time avoid them, he would lob great artillery shells of goodness at them. Under cover of the smoke he would beat his retreat.

In the face of his goodness, Irena was at first

27

unsettled, confused: why was he so kind, so generous, so undemanding? How could she repay him? The only recompense she could figure out was to display her desire. She would set her wide-eyed gaze on him, a gaze that demanded some immense, intoxicating, nameless thing.

Her desire; the sad story of her desire. She had never known sexual pleasure before she met Martin. Then she bore a child, moved from Prague to France with a second daughter in her belly, and soon after that Martin was dead. She went through some long, hard years then, forced to take on any sort of work—cleaning houses, caring for a rich paraplegic—and it was a big triumph just to get the chance to do translations from Russian to French (she was glad to have studied languages seriously in Prague). The years rolled by, and on posters, on billboards, on the covers of magazines displayed on the newsstands, women stripped and couples kissed and men strutted in underpants, while amid the universal orgy her own body roamed the streets neglected and invisible.

So meeting Gustaf had been a festival. After such a long time, her body, her face were finally being seen and appreciated, and because they

28

were pleasing, a man had invited her to share life with him. It was in the midst of that enchantment that her mother turned up in Paris. But at perhaps that same time, or very slightly later, she began to harbor a vague suspicion that her body had not entirely escaped the fate it was apparently destined for all along. That Gustaf, who was fleeing his wife, his women, was looking to her not for an adventure, a new youth, a freedom of the senses, but for a rest. Let's not exaggerate; her body did not go untouched; but her suspicion grew that it was being touched less than it deserved.

8

Europe's Communism burned out exactly two hundred years after the French Revolution took fire. For Irena's Parisian friend Sylvie, that was a coincidence loaded with meaning. But with what meaning? What name could be given to the triumphal arch spanning those two majestic dates? *The Arch of the Two Greatest European Revolu-*

tions? Or *The Arch Connecting the Greatest Rev-olution with the Final Restoration?* For the sake of avoiding ideological argument, I propose that we adopt a more modest interpretation: the first date gave birth to a great European character, the Émigré (either the Great Traitor or the Great Victim, according to one's outlook); the second date took the Émigré off the set of The History of the Europeans; with that, the great moviemaker of the collective unconscious finished off one of his most original productions, the emigration-dream show. And it was at this moment that Irena first returned to Prague for a few days.

When she set out it was very cold, and then after she had been there three days, summer arrived suddenly, unexpectedly, unseasonably. Her thick suit became unwearable. Having packed nothing for warmer weather, she went to a shop to buy a summer dress. The country was not yet overflowing with merchandise from the West, and all she found was the same fabrics, the same colors, the same styles she had known during the Communist period. She tried on two or three dresses and was uncomfortable. Hard to say why: they weren't ugly, their cut wasn't bad, but they reminded her of her distant past, the sartorial austerity of her youth; they looked naive, provincial, inelegant, fit for a country schoolteacher. But she was in a hurry. Why, after all, shouldn't she look like a country schoolteacher for a few days? She bought the dress for a ridiculous price, kept it on, and with her winter suit in the bag stepped out into the hot street.

Then, walking by a big department store, she unexpectedly passed a wall covered with an enormous mirror and she was stunned: the person she saw was not she, it was somebody else or, when she looked longer at herself in her new dress, it was she but she living a different life, the life she would have lived if she had stayed in Prague. This woman was not dislikable, she was even touching, but a little too touching, touching to the point of tears, pitiable, poor, weak, downtrodden.

She was gripped by the same panic she used to feel in her emigration-dreams: through the magical power of a dress she could see herself imprisoned in a life she did not want and would never again be able to leave. As if long ago, at the start of her adult life, she had had a choice among several possible lives and had ended up choosing the one that took her to France. And as if those other lives, rejected and abandoned, were still lying in wait for her and were jealously watching for her from their lairs. One of them had now snatched Irena and bound her into her new dress as if into a straitjacket.

Frightened, she hurried home to Gustaf's apartment (his company had bought a house in central Prague and he kept a pied-à-terre up under the eaves) and changed her clothes. Back in her winter suit now, she looked out the window. The sky was cloudy, and the trees bent under the wind. It had been hot for only a few hours. A few hours of heat to play a nightmare trick on her, to call up the horror of the return.

(Was it a dream? Her final emigration-dream? No, no, the whole thing today had been real. Still, she had the sense that the snares she knew from those early dreams were not done with—that they were still present, still at the ready, on the lookout for her.)

9

During the twenty years of Odysseus' absence, the people of Ithaca retained many recollections of him but never felt nostalgia for him. Whereas Odysseus did suffer nostalgia, and remembered almost nothing.

We can comprehend this curious contradiction if we realize that for memory to function well, it needs constant practice: if recollections are not evoked again and again, in conversations with friends, they go. Émigrés gathered together in compatriot colonies keep retelling to the point of nausea the same stories, which thereby become unforgettable. But people who do not spend time with their compatriots, like Irena or Odysseus, are inevitably stricken with amnesia. The stronger their nostalgia, the emptier of recollections it becomes. The more Odysseus languished, the more he forgot. For nostalgia does not heighten memory's activity, it does not awaken recollections; it suffices unto itself, unto its own feelings, so fully absorbed is it by its suffering and nothing else.

After killing off the brazen fellows who hoped to marry Penelope and rule Ithaca, Odysseus was obliged to live with people he knew nothing about. To flatter him they would go over and over everything they could recall about him before he left for the war. And because they believed that all he was interested in was his Ithaca (how could they think otherwise, since he had journeyed over the immensity of the seas to get back to the place?), they nattered on about things that had happened during his absence, eager to answer any question he might have. Nothing bored him more. He was waiting for just one thing: for them finally to say "Tell us!" And that is the one thing they never said.

For twenty years he had thought about nothing but his return. But once he was back, he was amazed to realize that his life, the very essence of his life, its center, its treasure, lay outside Ithaca, in the twenty years of his wanderings. And this treasure he had lost, and could retrieve only by telling about it.

After leaving Calypso, during his return journey, he was shipwrecked in Phaeacia, whose king welcomed him to his court. There he was a foreigner, a mysterious stranger. A stranger gets asked "Who are you? Where do you come from? Tell us!" and he had told. For four long books of the *Odyssey* he had retraced in detail his adventures before the dazzled Phaeacians. But in Ithaca he was not a stranger, he was one of their own, so it never occurred to anyone to say, "Tell us!"

10

She leafed through her old address books, lingering over half-forgotten names; then she reserved a room at a restaurant. On a long table against the wall, alongside platters of petits fours, twelve bottles stood in neat rows. In Bohemia people don't drink good wine, and there is no custom of laying down vintage bottlings. She bought this old Bordeaux with all the greater pleasure: to surprise her guests, to make a party for them, to regain their friendship.

She came close to ruining it all. Awkwardly her friends eye the bottles until one of them, full of confidence and proud of her plain-and-simple style, declares her preference for beer. Emboldened anew by this outspokenness, the others go along and the beer lover calls the waiter.

Irena blames herself for having committed an act of poor taste with her case of Bordeaux, for thoughtlessly underscoring everything that stands between them: her long absence from the country, her foreigner's ways, her wealth. She blames herself the more because the gathering is so important for her: she hopes finally to figure out whether she can live here, feel at home, have friends. So she determines not to let that bit of boorishness bother her, she is even willing to see it as a pleasing directness; after all, this beer her guests are so loyal to, isn't beer the holy libation of sincerity? the potion that dispels all hypocrisy, any charade of fine manners? the drink that does nothing worse than incite its fans to urinate in all innocence, to gain weight in all frankness? And in fact the women in the room are fullheartedly fat, they talk incessantly, overflow with good advice, and sing the praises of Gustaf, whose existence they all know about.

Meanwhile, the waiter appears in the doorway with ten half-liter mugs of beer, five in each hand, a great athletic feat that provokes applause and laughter. They all lift their mugs and toast: "Health to Irena! Health to the daughter who's returned!"

Irena takes a small sip of beer, thinking: And suppose it were Gustaf offering them the wine? Would they have turned it down? Certainly not. Rejecting the wine was rejecting her. Her as the person she is now, coming back after so many years.

And that was exactly her gamble: that they'd accept her as the person she is now, coming back. She left here as a naive young woman, and she has come back mature, with a life behind her, a difficult life that she's proud of. She means to do all she can to get them to accept her with her experiences of the past twenty years, with her convictions, her ideas; it'll be double or nothing: either she succeeds in being among them as the person she has become, or else she won't stay. She arranged this gathering as the starting point in her campaign. They can drink beer if they insist, that doesn't faze her; what matters to her is choosing the topic of conversation herself and being heard.

But time is passing, the women are all talking at once, and it is nearly impossible to have a conversation, much less to impose its subject. She tries delicately to take up topics they raise and lead them toward what she wants to tell them, but she fails: as soon as her remarks move away from their own concerns, no one listens.

The waiter has already brought the second round of beer; her first mug is still standing on the table with its foam collapsed as if disgraced alongside the exuberant foam of the fresh mug. Irena faults herself for having lost her taste for beer; in France she learned to savor a drink by small mouthfuls, and is no longer used to bolting great quantities of liquid as beer-loving requires. She raises the mug to her lips and forces herself to take two, three swigs in a row. Just then one woman—the oldest of them all, about sixty—gently puts her hand to Irena's lips and wipes away the flecks of foam left there.

"Don't force yourself," she tells her. "Suppose we have a little wine ourselves? It would be idiotic to pass up such a good wine," and she asks the waiter to open one of the bottles still standing untouched on the long table.

11

Milada had been a colleague of Martin's, working at the same institute. Irena had recognized her when she first appeared at the door of the room, but only now, each of them with a wine glass in hand, is she able to talk to her. She looks at her: Milada still has the same shape face (round), the same dark hair, the same hairstyle (also round, covering the ears and falling to below the chin). She appears not to have changed; however, when she begins to speak, her face is abruptly transformed: her skin creases and creases again, her upper lip shows fine vertical lines, while wrinkles on her cheeks and chin shift rapidly with every expression. Irena thinks Milada certainly must not realize this: people don't talk to themselves in front of a mirror; she would see her own face only when it is at rest, with the skin nearly smooth; every mirror in the world would have her believe that she is still beautiful.

As she savors the wine, Milada says (and instantly, on her lovely face, the wrinkles spring forth and start to dance): "It's not easy, returning, is it?"

39

"They can't understand that we left without the slightest hope of coming back. We did our best to drop anchor where we were. Do you know Skacel?"

"The poet?"

"There's a stanza where he talks about his sadness; he says he wants to build a house out of it and lock himself inside for three hundred years. Three hundred years. We all saw a three-hundred-year-long tunnel stretching ahead of us."

"Sure, we did too, here."

"So then why isn't anyone willing to acknowledge that?"

"Because people revise their feelings if the feelings were wrong. If history has disproved them."

"And then, too: everybody thinks we left to get ourselves an easy life. They don't know how hard it is to carve out a little place for yourself in a foreign world. Can you imagine—leaving your country with a baby and with another one in your belly. Losing your husband. Raising your two daughters with no money . . ."

She falls silent, and Milada says: "It makes no sense to tell them all that. Even until just lately, everybody was arguing about who had the hardest time under the old regime. Everybody wanted to be acknowledged as a victim. But those suffering-contests are over now. These days people brag about success, not about suffering. So if they're prepared to respect you now, it's not for the hard life you've had, it's because they see you've got yourself a rich man!"

They've been talking for a long time in a corner when the other women approach and collect around them. As if to make up for not paying enough attention to their hostess, they are garrulous (a beer high makes people more noisy and good-humored than a wine high) and affectionate. The woman who earlier had demanded beer cries: "I've really got to taste your wine!" and she calls the waiter, who opens more bottles and fills glasses.

Irena is gripped by a sudden vision: beer mugs in hand and laughing noisily, a bunch of women rush up to her, she makes out Czech words, and understands, horrified, that she is not in France, that she is in Prague and she is doomed. Oh, yes—it's one of her old emigration-dreams, and she quickly banishes the memory of it: in fact the women around her aren't drinking beer now,

41

they're raising wineglasses, and again they're toasting the daughter's return; then one of them, beaming, says to her: "You remember? I wrote you that it was high time, high time you came back!"

Who is that woman? The whole evening she's been talking about her husband's sickness, lingering excitedly over all the morbid details. Finally Irena recognizes her: the high-school classmate who wrote her the very week Communism fell: "Oh, my dear, we're old already! It's high time you came back!" Again, now, she repeats that line, and in her thickened face a broad grin reveals dentures.

The other women assail her with questions: "Irena, remember when . . . ?" And "You know what happened back then with . . . ?" "Oh, no, really, you must remember him!" "That guy with the big ears, you always made fun of him!" "No, you can't possibly have forgotten him! You're all he talks about!"

Until that moment they have shown no interest in what she was trying to tell them. What is the meaning of this sudden onslaught? What is it they want to find out, these women who wouldn't listen to anything before? She soon sees that their questions are of a particular kind: questions to check whether she knows what they know, whether she remembers what they remember. This has a strange effect on her, one that will stay with her:

Earlier, by their total uninterest in her experience abroad, they amputated twenty years from her life. Now, with this interrogation, they are trying to stitch her old past onto her present life. As if they were amputating her forearm and attaching the hand directly to the elbow; as if they were amputating her calves and joining her feet to her knees.

Transfixed by that image, she can give no answer to their questions; anyhow, the women are not expecting one, and, drunker and drunker, they fall back into their chatter, which leaves Irena out. She watches their mouths opening all at the same time, mouths moving and emitting words and constantly bursting into laughter (a mystery: how is it that women not listening to one another can laugh at what the others are saying?). None of them is talking to Irena anymore, but they're all beaming with good humor, the woman who started off by ordering beer begins singing, the others do the same, and even when the party's over, they go on singing out in the street.

In bed Irena thinks back over her party; once again her old emigration-dream comes back and she sees herself surrounded by women, noisy and hearty, raising their beer mugs. In the dream they were working for the secret police with orders to entrap her. But for whom were tonight's women working? "It's high time you came back," said her old classmate with the macabre dentures. As an emissary from the graveyards (the graveyards of the homeland), her job was to call Irena back into line: to warn her that time is short and that life is supposed to finish up where it started.

Then her thoughts turn to Milada, who was so maternally friendly; she made it clear that nobody is interested anymore in Irena's odyssey, and Irena realizes that, actually, neither is Milada. But how can she blame her? Why should Milada be interested in something that has no connection at all with her own life? It would be just a polite charade, and Irena is glad that Milada was so kindly, with no charade.

Her last thought before sleeping is about Sylvie. It's already so long since she's seen her! She misses her! Irena would love to take her out to their Paris bistro and tell her all about her recent trip to Bohemia. Get her to understand how hard it is to return home. Actually you were the first, she imagines telling her, the first person who used those words: the Great Return. And you know something, Sylvie—now I understand: I could go back and live with them, but there'd be a condition: I'd have to lay my whole life with you, with all of you, with the French, solemnly on the altar of the homeland and set fire to it. Twenty years of my life spent abroad would go up in smoke, in a sacrificial ceremony. And the women would sing and dance with me around the fire, with beer mugs raised high in their hands. That's the price I'd have to pay to be pardoned. To be accepted. To become one of them again.

12

One day at the Paris airport, she moved through the police checkpoint and sat down to wait for the Prague flight. On the facing bench she saw a man and, after a few moments of uncertainty and sur-

prise, she recognized him. In excitement she
waited till their glances met, and then she smiled.
He smiled back and nodded slightly. She rose and
crossed to him as he rose in turn.

"Didn't we know each other in Prague?" she
said in Czech. "Do you still remember me?"

"Of course."

"I recognized you right away. You haven't
changed."

"Oh, that's an exaggeration."

"No, no. You look just the same. Good Lord, it's
all so long ago." Then, laughing: "I'm grateful to
you for recognizing me!" And then: "You've
stayed there all that time?"

"No."

"You emigrated?"

"Yes."

"And where've you been living? In France?"

"No."

She sighed: "Ah, if you'd been living in France
and we're only running into each other now . . ."

"It's pure chance that I'm going through Paris.
I live in Denmark. What about you?"

"Here. In Paris. Good Lord. I can hardly
believe my eyes. What have you been doing all

this time? Have you been able to carry on with your work?"

"Yes. What about you?"

"I must have done about seven different things."

"I won't ask you how many men you've been with."

"No, don't. And I promise not to ask you that kind of question either."

"And now? You've gone back?"

"Not completely. I still have my apartment in Paris. What about you?"

"Neither have I."

"But you do return often."

"No. This is the first time," he said.

"Oh, so late! You were in no big rush!"

"No."

"You have no obligations in Bohemia?"

"I'm a completely free man."

His tone was even, and she noted some melancholy as well.

Aboard the airplane her seat was forward on the aisle, and several times she turned to look back at him. She had never forgotten their long-ago encounter. It was in Prague, she was with a

47

bunch of friends in a bar, and he, a friend of one of them, never took his eyes off her. Their love story stopped before it could start. She still felt regret over it, a wound that never healed.

Twice she went to lean against his seat and continue their conversation. She learned that he would be in Bohemia for only three or four days, and at that in a provincial city to see his family. She was sad to hear it. Wouldn't he be in Prague for even a day? Well, yes, actually, on his way back to Denmark, maybe a day or two. Could she see him? It would be such a pleasure to get together again! He gave her the name of his hotel in the provinces.

13

He enjoyed the encounter, too; she was friendly, charming, and agreeable; forty-something and pretty; and he hadn't the faintest idea who she was. It's awkward to tell someone you don't remember her, but doubly awkward in this case because maybe it wasn't that he'd forgotten her but just that she didn't look the same. And to tell a woman that is too boorish for him. Besides, he saw right away that this unknown woman was not going to make an issue of whether or not he remembered her, and that it was the easiest thing in the world to chat with her. But when they agreed to meet again and she offered to give him her telephone number, he was flustered: how could he phone a person whose name he didn't know? Without explaining, he said he would rather she call him, and asked her to take down the number at his provincial hotel.

At the Prague airport they separated. He rented a car, took the expressway and then a local highway. When he reached the city, he looked for the cemetery. But in vain. He found himself in a new neighborhood of tall identical buildings that threw him off. He spotted a boy of about ten, stopped the car, asked the way to the cemetery. The boy stared at him without answering. Thinking he had not understood, Josef articulated his question more slowly, louder, like a foreigner trying to enunciate clearly. The boy finally answered that he didn't know. But how in hell can a person not know where the cemetery is, the only cemetery in town? Josef shifted gears, set off again, asked some other people, but their directions seemed barely intelligible. Eventually he found it: cramped behind a newly built viaduct, it seemed unimposing, and much smaller than it used to be.

He parked the car and walked down a lane of linden trees to the grave. Here, some thirty years earlier, he had watched the lowering of the coffin that held his mother. He had often come here afterward, on every visit to his hometown before his departure abroad. When, a month ago, he was planning this trip back to Bohemia, he already knew he would begin it here. He looked at the tombstone; the marble was covered with many names: apparently the grave had meanwhile become a large dormitory. Between the lane and the tombstone there was only lawn, neatly kept, with a flowerbed; he tried to imagine the coffins underneath: they must lie jammed one against the next, in rows of three, piled several layers deep. Mama was way down at the bottom. Where was the father? He had died fifteen years later; he would be separated from her by at least one layer of coffins.

He envisioned Mama's burial again. At the

time there were only two bodies in the grave: his father's parents. He'd found it perfectly natural back then that his mother should be with her husband's family; he'd never even wondered if she might not have preferred to join her own parents. Only later did he understand: regroupings in family vaults are determined well in advance by power relationships; his father's family was more influential than his mother's.

The number of new names on the stone troubled him. A few years after he left the country, he got word of his uncle's death, then of his aunt's, then eventually of his father's. Now he began reading the names closely; some were of people he had thought still living; he was stunned. It was not their deaths that unsettled him (anyone who decides to leave his country forever has to resign himself never to see his family again), but the fact that he had not been sent any announcement. The Communist police kept watch on letters addressed to émigrés; had people been afraid to write him? He examined the dates: the two most recent were after 1989. So it was not out of caution that they didn't write. The truth was worse: he no longer existed for them.

14

The hotel dated from the last years of Communism: a sleek modern building of the sort built all over the world, on the main square, very tall, towering by many stories over the city's rooftops. He settled into his seventh-floor room and then went to the window. It was seven in the evening, dusk was falling, the streetlights went on, and the square was amazingly quiet.

Before leaving Denmark he had considered the coming encounter with places he had known, with his past life, and had wondered: would he be moved? cold? delighted? depressed? Nothing of the sort. During his absence, an invisible broom had swept across the landscape of his childhood, wiping away everything familiar; the encounter he had expected never took place.

A long time ago Irena had visited a town in the French provinces, seeking out a little respite for her husband, who was already very ill. It was a Sunday; the town was quiet; they stopped on a bridge and stared at the water flowing peacefully between the greenish banks. At the point where the river formed an elbow, an old villa surrounded by a garden looked to them like the image of a comforting home, the dream of an idyll long past. Caught up by the beauty, they took a stairway down onto the embankment, hoping for a stroll. After a few steps they saw that they'd been fooled by the Sunday peacefulness; the way was barricaded; they came up against an abandoned construction site: machines, tractors, mounds of earth and sand; on the far side of the river, trees lay felled; and the villa whose beauty had drawn them when they saw it from above now revealed broken windowpanes and a huge hole in place of a front door; behind the house jutted a building project ten stories high; yet the cityscape's beauty that had struck them with wonder was not an optical illusion; trampled, humiliated, mocked, it still showed through its own ruin. Irena looked again at the far bank and she saw that the great felled trees were in flower! Felled and laid out flat, they were alive! Just then music suddenly exploded from a loudspeaker, fortissimo. At that bludgeoning Irena clapped her hands over her ears and burst into sobs. Sobs for the world that was vanishing before her eyes. Her husband, who was to die in a few months, took her by the hand and led her away.

The gigantic invisible broom that transforms, disfigures, erases landscapes has been at the job for millennia now, but its movements, which used to be slow, just barely perceptible, have sped up so much that I wonder: Would an *Odyssey* even be conceivable today? Is the epic of the return still pertinent to our time? When Odysseus woke on Ithaca's shore that morning, could he have listened in ecstasy to the music of the Great Return if the old olive tree had been felled and he recognized nothing around him?

Near the hotel a tall building exposed its bare side, a blind wall decorated with a gigantic picture. In the twilight the caption was unreadable, and all Josef could make out was two hands clasping, enormous hands, between sky and earth. Had they always been there? He couldn't recall.

He was dining alone at the hotel restaurant and all around him he heard the sound of conversations. It was the music of some unknown language. What had happened to Czech during those two sorry decades? Was it the stresses that had changed? Apparently. Hitherto set firmly on the first syllable, they had grown weaker; the intonation seemed boneless. The melody sounded more monotone than before—drawling. And the timbre! It had turned nasal, which gave the speech an unpleasantly blasé quality. Over the centuries the music of any language probably does change imperceptibly, but to a person returning after an absence it can be disconcerting: bent over his plate, Josef was listening to an unknown language whose every word he understood.

Then, in his room, he picked up the telephone and dialed his brother's number. He heard a joyful voice inviting him to come over right away.

"I just wanted to tell you I'm here," said Josef. "Do excuse me for today, though. I don't want you to see me like this after all these years. I'm knocked out. Are you free tomorrow?"

He wasn't even sure his brother still worked at the hospital.

"I'll get free," was the answer.

15

He rings, and his brother, five years older than he, opens the door. They grip hands and gaze at each other. These are gazes of enormous intensity, and both men know very well what is going on: they are registering—swiftly, discreetly, brother about brother—the hair, the wrinkles, the teeth; each knows what he is looking for in the face before him, and each knows that the other is looking for the same thing in his. They are ashamed of doing so, because what they're looking for is the probable distance between the other man and death or, to say it more bluntly, each is looking in the other man's face for death beginning to show through. To put a quick end to that morbid scrutiny, they cast about for some phrase to make them forget those few grievous seconds, some exclamation or question, or if possible (it would be a gift from heaven) a joke (but nothing comes to their rescue).

"Come," the brother finally says and, taking Josef by the shoulders, leads him into the living room.

16

"We've been expecting you ever since the thing collapsed," the brother said when they sat down. "All the émigrés have already come home, or at least put in an appearance. No, no, that's not a reproach. You know best what's right for you."

"There you're wrong," said Josef with a laugh. "I don't know that."

"Did you come alone?" the brother asked.

"Yes."

"Are you thinking of moving back for good?"

"I don't know."

"Of course you'd have to take your wife's feelings into consideration. You got married over there, I believe."

"Yes."

"To a Danish woman," said his brother, hesitantly.

"Yes," Josef said, and did not go on.

The silence made the brother uncomfortable, and just to say something, Josef asked, "The house belongs to you now?"

In the old days the apartment had been part of

a three-story income property belonging to their father; the family (father, mother, two sons) lived on the top floor and the other two were rented out. After the Communist revolution of 1948 the house was expropriated, and the family stayed on as tenant.

"Yes," answered the brother, visibly embarrassed. "We tried to get in touch with you, but we couldn't."

"Why was that? You do know my address!"

After 1989 all properties nationalized by the revolution (factories, hotels, rental apartments, land, forests) were returned to their former owners (or more precisely, to their children or grandchildren); the procedure was called "restitution": it required only that a person declare himself owner to the legal authorities, and after a year during which his claim might be contested, the restitution became irrevocable. That judicial simplification allowed for a good deal of fraud, but it did avoid inheritance disputes, lawsuits, appeals, and thus brought about, in an astonishingly short time, the rebirth of a class society with a bourgeoisie that was rich, entrepreneurial, and positioned to set the national economy going.

"There was a lawyer handling it," answered the brother, still embarrassed. "Now it's already too late. The proceedings are closed now. But don't worry, we'll work things out between us and with no lawyers involved."

Just then the sister-in-law came in. This time that collision of gazes never even occurred: she had aged so much that the whole story was clear from the moment she appeared in the doorway. Josef wanted to drop his eyes and only look at her later, secretly, so as not to upset her. Stricken with pity, he stood up, went to her, and embraced her.

They sat down again. Unable to shake free of his emotion, Josef looked at her; if he had met her in the street, he would not have recognized her. These are the people who are closest to me in the world, he told himself, my family, all the family I have, my brother, my only brother. He repeated these words to himself as if to make the most of his emotion before it should dissipate.

That wave of tenderness caused him to say: "Forget the house business completely. Listen, really, let's be pragmatic—owning something here is not my problem. My problems aren't here."

Relieved, the brother repeated: "No, no. I like equity in everything. Besides, your wife should have her say on the subject."

"Let's talk about something else," Josef said as he laid his hand on his brother's and squeezed it.

17

They took him through the apartment to show him the changes since he had left. In one room he saw a painting that had belonged to him. When he'd decided to leave the country, he had to act quickly. He was living in another town at the time, and since he needed to keep secret his intention to emigrate, he could not give himself away by doling out his possessions to friends. The night before he left, he had put his keys in an envelope and mailed them to his brother. Then he'd phoned him from abroad and asked him to take anything he liked from the apartment before the state confiscated it. Later on, living in Denmark and happy to be starting a new life, he hadn't the slightest desire to find out what his brother had managed to salvage and what he had done with it.

He gazed for a long while at the picture: a working-class suburb, poor, rendered in that bold welter of colors that recalled the Fauve artists from the turn of the century, Derain for example. And yet the painting was no pastiche; if it had been shown in 1905 at the Salon d'Automne together with works by the Fauves, viewers would have been struck by its strangeness, intrigued by the enigmatic perfume of an alluring visitor come from some faraway place. In fact the picture was painted in 1955, a period when doctrine on socialist art was strict in its demand for realism: this artist, who was a passionate modernist, would have preferred to paint the way people were painting all over the world at the time, which is to say in the abstract manner, but he also wanted his work to be exhibited; therefore he had to locate the magic point where the ideologues' imperatives intersected with his own desires as an artist; the shacks evoking workers' lives were a bow to the ideologues, and the violently unrealistic colors were his gift to himself.

Josef had visited the man's studio in the 1960s,

when the official doctrine was losing some of its force and the painter was already free to do pretty much whatever he wanted. In his naive sincerity Josef had liked this early picture better than the recent ones, and the painter, who looked on his own proletarian Fauvism with a slightly condescending affection, had cheerfully made him a gift of it; he'd even picked up his brush and, alongside his signature, written a dedication with Josef's name.

"You knew this painter well," remarked the brother.

"Yes. I saved his poodle's life for him."

"Are you planning to go see him?"

"No."

Shortly after 1989 a package had arrived at Josef's house in Denmark: photographs of the painter's latest canvases, created now in complete freedom. They were indistinguishable from the millions of other pictures being painted around the planet at the time; the painter could boast of a double victory: he was utterly free and utterly like everybody else.

"You still like this picture?" asked the brother.

"Yes, it's still very fine."

The brother tilted his head toward his wife: "Katy loves it. She stops to look at it every day." Then he added: "After you left, you told me to give it to Papa. He hung it over the table in his office at the hospital. He knew how much Katy loved it, and before he died he bequeathed it to her." After a little pause: "You can't imagine. We lived through some dreadful years."

Looking at the sister-in-law, Josef remembered that he had never liked her. His old antipathy (she'd returned it in spades) now seemed to him stupid and regrettable. She stood there staring at the picture with an expression of sad impotence on her face, and in pity Josef said to his brother: "I know."

The brother began an account of the family's story: the father's lingering death, Katy's illness, their daughter's failed marriage, then on to the cabals against him at the hospital, where his position had been gravely compromised by the fact of Josef's emigrating.

There was no tone of reproach to that last remark, but Josef had no doubt of the animosity with which the brother and sister-in-law must have discussed him at the time, indignant at the paltry reasons Josef might have alleged to justify his emigration, which they certainly considered irresponsible: the regime did not make life easy for the relatives of émigrés.

18

In the dining room the table was set for lunch. The conversation turned lively, with the brother and sister-in-law eager to inform him of every-thing that had happened during his absence. The decades hovered above the dishes, and his sister-in-law suddenly attacked him: "You had some fanatical years yourself. The way you used to talk about the Church! We were all scared of you."

The remark startled him. "Scared of me?" His sister-in-law held her ground. He looked at her: on her face, which only minutes earlier had seemed unrecognizable, her old features were coming out.

To say that they'd been scared of him was non-sense, actually, since the sister-in-law's recollection could only concern his high-school years, when he was between sixteen and nineteen years old. It is entirely possible that he used to make fun of believers back then, but his taunts couldn't have been anything like the government's militant atheism and were meant only for his family, who never missed Sunday Mass and thereby incited Josef to be provocative. He had graduated in 1951, three years after the revolution, and when he decided to study veterinary medicine it was that same taste for provocation that inspired him: healing sick people, serving humanity, was his family's great pride (already two generations back, his grandfather had been a doctor), and he enjoyed telling them all that he liked cows better than humans. But nobody had either praised or deplored his rebellion; because veterinary medicine carried less social prestige, his choice was interpreted simply as a lack of ambition, an acceptance of second rank within the family, below his brother.

Now at the table he made a garbled effort to explain (to them and to himself both) his psychology as an adolescent, but the words had trouble getting out of his mouth because the sister-in-law's set smile, fastened on him, expressed an immutable disagreement with everything he was saying. He understood that there was nothing he could do about it; it was practically a law: People who see their lives as a shipwreck set out to hunt down the guilty parties. And Josef was doubly guilty: both as an adolescent who had spoken ill of God and as an adult who had emigrated. He lost the desire to explain anything at all, and his brother, subtle diplomat that he was, changed the subject.

His brother: as a second-year medical student, he had been barred from the university in 1948 because of his bourgeois background; so as not to lose hope of resuming his studies later on and becoming a surgeon like his father, he had done all he could to demonstrate his support for Communism, to the point where one day, sore at heart, he wound up joining the Party, in which he stayed until 1989. The paths of the two brothers diverged: first ejected from school and then forced to deny his convictions, the elder felt himself a victim (he would feel that way forever); at the veterinary school, which was less coveted and less tightly monitored, the younger brother had no need to display any particular loyalty to the regime: to his brother he seemed (and forever would seem) a lucky little bastard who knew how to get away with things; a deserter.

In August 1968 the Russian army had invaded the country; for a week the streets in all the cities howled with rage. The country had never been so thoroughly a homeland, or the Czechs so Czech. Drunk with hatred, Josef was ready to hurl himself against the tanks. Then the country's statesmen were arrested, shipped under guard to Moscow, and forced to conclude a slapdash compromise, and the Czechs, still enraged, went back indoors. Some fourteen months later, on the fifty-second anniversary of Russia's October Revolution, imposed on the country as a national holiday, Josef had climbed into his car in the town where he had his animal clinic and set off to see his family at the other end of the country. Arriving in their city, he slowed down; he was curious to see how many windows would be draped with red flags which, in that year of defeat, were nothing else but signals of submission. There were more of them than he expected: perhaps the people displaying them were doing so against their actual convictions, out of prudence, with some

vague fear; still, they were acting voluntarily, no
one was forcing them, no one was threatening
them. He had pulled up in front of his family
home. On the top floor, where his brother lived,
there blazed a large flag, hideously red. For a very
long moment Josef contemplated it from inside
his car; then he turned on the ignition. On the trip
home he decided to leave the country. Not that he
couldn't have lived here. He could have gone on
peacefully treating cows here. But he was alone,
divorced, childless, free. He reflected that he had
only one life and that he wanted to live it somewhere else.

19

At the end of lunch, sitting over his coffee, Josef
thought about his painting. He considered how to
take it away with him, and whether it would be
too unwieldy in the airplane. Wouldn't it be easier
to take the canvas out of the frame and roll it up?

He was about to discuss it when the sister-in-
law said: "You must be going to see N."

"I don't know yet."

"He was an awfully good friend of yours."

"He still is my friend."

"In 'forty-eight everyone was terrified of him. The Red Commissar! But he did a lot for you, didn't he? You owe him!"

The brother hastily interrupted his wife, and he handed Josef a small bundle: "This is what Papa kept as a souvenir of you. We found it after he died."

The brother apparently had to leave soon for the hospital; their meeting was drawing to a close, and Josef noted that his painting had vanished from the conversation. What? His sister-in-law remembers his friend N., but she forgets his painting? Still, although he was prepared to give up his whole inheritance, and his share of the house, the picture was his, his alone, with his name inscribed alongside the painter's! How could they, she and his brother, act as if it didn't belong to him?

The atmosphere suddenly grew heavy, and the brother started to tell a funny story. Josef was not listening. He was determined to reclaim his picture, and, intent on what he wanted to say, his distracted glance fell on the brother's wrist and the watch on it. He recognized it: big and black, a little out of style; he had left it behind in his apartment and the brother had appropriated it for himself. No, Josef had no reason to be incensed at that. It had all been done according to his own instructions; still, seeing his watch on someone else's wrist threw him into a strange unease. He had the sense he was coming back into the world as might a dead man emerging from his tomb after twenty years: touching the ground with a timid foot that's lost the habit of walking; barely recognizing the world he had lived in but continually stumbling over the leavings from his life; seeing his trousers, his tie on the bodies of the survivors, who had quite naturally divided them up among themselves; seeing everything and laying claim to nothing: the dead are timid. Overcome by that timidity of the dead, Josef could not summon the strength to say a single word about his painting. He stood up.

"Come back tonight. We'll have dinner together," said the brother.

Josef suddenly saw his own wife's face; he felt a sharp need to address her, talk with her. But he could not do that: his brother was looking at him, waiting for his answer.

"Please excuse me, I have so little time. Next visit," and he gave them each a warm handshake.

On the way back to the hotel, his wife's face appeared to him again and he blew up: "It's your fault. You're the one who told me I had to go. I didn't want to. I had no desire for this return. But you disagreed. You said that not going was unnatural, unjustifiable, it was even foul. Do you still think you were right?"

20

Back in his hotel room, he opens the bundle his brother gave him: an album of photographs from his childhood, of his mother, his father, his brother, and, many times over, little Josef; he sets it aside to keep. A couple of children's picture books; he tosses them into the wastebasket. A child's drawing in colored pencil, with the inscription "For Mama on her birthday" and his clumsy signature; he tosses that away. Then a notebook.

He opens it: his high-school diary. How did he ever leave that at his parents' house?

The entries dated from the early years of Communism here, but, his curiosity somewhat foiled, he finds only accounts of his dates with girls from high school. A precocious libertine? No indeed: a virgin boy. He leafs through the pages absently, then stops at these rebukes addressed to one girl: "You told me love was only about bodies. Dear girl, you would run off in a minute if a man told you he was only interested in your body. And you would come to understand the dreadful sensation of loneliness."

"Loneliness." The word keeps turning up in these pages. He would try to scare them by describing the fearsome prospect of loneliness. To make them love him, he would preach at them like a parson that unless there's emotion, sex stretches away like a desert where a person can die of sadness.

He goes on reading, and remembers nothing. So what has this stranger come to tell him? To remind him that he used to live here under Josef's name? Josef gets up and goes to the window. The square is lit by the late-afternoon sun, and the image of the two hands on the big wall is sharply visible now: one is white, the other black. Above them a three-letter acronym promises "security" and "solidarity." No doubt about it, the mural was painted after 1989, when the country took up the slogans of the new age: brotherhood of all races; mingling of all cultures; unity of everything, of everybody.

Hands clasping on billboards, Josef's seen that before! The Czech worker clasping the hand of the Russian soldier! It may have been detested, but that propaganda image was indisputably part of the history of the Czechs, who had a thousand reasons to clasp or to refuse the hands of Russians or Germans! But a black hand? In this country, people hardly knew that blacks even existed. In her whole life his mother had never run into a single one.

He considers those hands suspended there between heaven and earth, enormous, taller than the church belfry, hands that shifted the place into a harshly different setting. He scrutinizes the square below him as if he were searching for traces he left on the pavement as a young man when he used to stroll it with his schoolmates.

"Schoolmates"; he articulates the word slowly, in an undertone, so as to breathe in the aroma (faint! barely perceptible!) of his early youth, that bygone, remote period, a period forsaken and mournful as an orphanage; but unlike Irena in the French country town, he feels no affection for that dimly visible, feeble past; no desire to return; nothing but a slight reserve; detachment.

If I were a doctor, I would diagnose his condition thus: "The patient is suffering from nostalgic insufficiency."

21

But Josef does not feel sick. He feels clearheaded. To his mind the nostalgic insufficiency proves the paltry value of his former life. So I revise my diagnosis: "The patient is suffering from masochistic distortion of memory." Indeed, all he remembers are situations that make him displeased with himself. He is not fond of his childhood. But as a child, didn't he have everything he wanted? Wasn't his father worshipped by all his patients? Why was that a source of pride for his brother and not for him? He often fought with his little pals, and he fought bravely. Now he's forgotten all his victories, but he will always remember the time a fellow he considered weaker than himself knocked him down and pinned him to the ground for a loud count of ten. Even now he can feel on his skin that humiliating pressure of the turf. When he was still living in Bohemia and would run into people who had known him earlier, he was always surprised to find that they considered him a fairly courageous person (he thought himself cowardly), with a caustic wit (he considered himself a bore) and a kind heart (he remembered only his stinginess).

He knew very well that his memory detested him, that it did nothing but slander him; therefore he tried not to believe it and to be more lenient toward his own life. But that didn't help: he took no pleasure in looking back, and he did it as seldom as possible.

What he would have other people, and himself, believe is that he left his country because he could not bear to see it enslaved and humiliated. That's true; still, most Czechs felt the same way, enslaved and humiliated, and yet they did not run off abroad. They stayed in their country because they liked themselves and because they liked themselves together with their lives, which were inseparable from the place where the lives had been lived. Because Josef's memory was malevolent and provided him nothing to make him cherish his life in his country, he crossed the border with a brisk step and with no regrets.

And once he was abroad, did his memory lose its noxious influence? Yes; because there Josef had neither reason nor occasion to concern himself with recollections bound to the country he no longer lived in; such is the law of masochistic memory: as segments of their lives melt into oblivion, men slough off whatever they dislike, and feel lighter, freer.

And above all, abroad Josef fell in love, and love is the glorification of the present. His attachment to the present drove off his recollections, shielded him against their intrusion; his memory did not become less malevolent but, disregarded and kept at a distance, it lost its power over him.

22

The more vast the amount of time we've left behind us, the more irresistible is the voice calling us to return to it. This pronouncement seems to state the obvious, and yet it is false. Men grow old, the end draws near, each moment becomes more and more valuable, and there is no time to waste over recollections. It is important to understand the mathematical paradox in nostalgia: that it is most powerful in early youth, when the volume of the life gone by is quite small.

Out of the mists of the time when Josef was in high school, I see a young girl emerge; she is long-limbed, beautiful; she is a virgin; and she is melancholy because she has just broken off with a boy. It is her first romantic separation and it hurts her, but her pain is less strong than her amazement at discovering time; she sees it as she never saw it before:

Until then her view of time was the present moving forward and devouring the future; she either feared its swiftness (when she was awaiting something difficult) or rebelled at its slowness (when she was awaiting something fine). Now time has a very different look; it is no longer the conquering present capturing the future; it is the present conquered and captured and carried off by the past. She sees a young man disconnecting himself from her life and going away, forevermore out of her reach. Mesmerized, all she can do is watch this piece of her life move off; all she can do is watch it and suffer. She is experiencing a brand-new feeling called nostalgia.

That feeling, that irrepressible yearning to return, suddenly reveals to her the existence of the past, the power of the past, of her past; in the house of her life there are windows now, windows opening to the rear, onto what she has experienced; from now on her existence will be inconceivable without these windows.

One day, with her new boyfriend (platonic, of course), she turns down a path in the forest near the town; it is the same path she had walked a few months earlier with her previous boyfriend (the one who, after their break, caused her to feel nostalgia for the first time), and she is moved by the coincidence. Deliberately she heads for a dilapidated little chapel at a crossing of the forest paths, because that was where her first boyfriend tried to kiss her. Irresistible temptation draws her to relive the bygone love. She wants the two love stories to come together, to join, to mingle, to mimic each other so that both will grow greater through their fusion.

When the earlier boyfriend had tried to stop at that spot and clasp her to him, happy and abashed she quickened her pace and prevented it. This time, what will happen? Her current boyfriend slows down too, he too prepares to take her in his arms! Dazzled by this repetition (by the miracle of this repetition), she obeys the imperative of the parallel and hurries ahead, pulling him along by the hand.

From then on she succumbs to the charm of these affinities, these furtive contacts between present and past; she seeks out these echoes, these co-respondences, these co-resonances that make her feel the distance between what was and what is, the temporal dimension (so new, so astonishing) of her life; she has the sense of emerging from adolescence because of it, of becoming mature, adult, which for her means becoming a person who is acquainted with time, who has left a fragment of life behind her and can turn to look back at it.

One day she sees her new boyfriend hurrying toward her in a blue jacket, and she remembers that her first boyfriend also looked good in a blue jacket. Another day, gazing into her eyes, he praises their beauty by way of a highly unusual metaphor; she was fascinated by that because her first boyfriend, commenting on her eyes, had used word for word the same unusual phrase. These coincidences amaze her. Never does she feel so thoroughly suffused with beauty as when the nostalgia for her past love blends with the surprises of her new love. The intrusion of the previous boyfriend into the story she is currently living is to her mind not some secret infidelity; it adds further to her fondness for the man walking beside her now.

When she is older she will see in these resemblances a regrettable uniformity among individuals (they all stop at the same spots to kiss, have the same tastes in clothing, flatter a woman with the same metaphor) and a tedious monotony among events (they are all just an endless repetition of the same one); but in her adolescence she welcomes these coincidences as miraculous and she is avid to decipher their meanings. The fact that today's boyfriend bears a strange resemblance to yesterday's makes him even more exceptional, even more original, and she believes that he is mysteriously predestined for her.

23

No, there is no allusion to politics in the diary. Not a trace of the period, except perhaps the puritanism of those early years of Communism, with the ideal of romantic love as backdrop. Josef is struck by a confession from the virgin boy: that he easily mustered the boldness to stroke a girl's breasts but he had to battle his own modesty to touch her rump. He had a good sense for exactness: "When we were together yesterday, I only dared to touch D.'s rump twice."

Intimidated by the rump, he was all the more avid for emotions: "She swears she loves me, her promise of intercourse is a victory for me . . ."

(apparently, intercourse as proof of love counted more for him than the physical act itself) ". . . but I feel let down: there is no ecstasy in our encounters. It terrifies me to imagine our life together." And farther along: "It's so tiring, faithfulness that does not spring from true passion."

"Ecstasy"; "life together"; "faithfulness"; "true passion." Josef lingers over these words. What could they have meant to an immature person? They were at the same time enormous and vague, and their power lay precisely in their nebulous nature. He was on a quest for sensations he had never experienced, did not understand; he was looking for them in his partner (on the watch for each little emotion her face might reflect), he looked for them in himself (for interminable hours of introspection), but he was always frustrated. At that point he wrote (and Josef has to acknowledge the startling perspicacity of this remark): "The desire to feel compassion for her and the desire to make her suffer are one and the same desire." And indeed he behaved as if he were guided by those words: in order to feel compassion (in order to reach the ecstasy of compassion), he did everything possible to see his girlfriend suffer; he tortured her: "I provoked her to doubts about my love. She fell into my arms, I consoled her, I wallowed in her sadness and, for a moment, I could feel a tiny flame of arousal flare up in me."

Josef tries to understand the virgin boy, to put himself in his skin, but he is not capable of it. That sentimentality mixed with sadism, that whole business is completely contrary to his tastes and to his nature. He tears a blank page out of the diary, picks up a pencil, and copies out the sentence "I wallowed in her sadness." He contemplates the two handwritings for a long time: the one from long ago is a little clumsy, but the letters are the same shape as today's. The resemblance is upsetting, it irritates him, it shocks him. How can two such alien, such opposite beings have the same handwriting? What common essence is it that makes a single person of him and this little snot?

24

Neither the virgin boy nor the high-school girl had access to an apartment to be alone in; the intercourse she promised him had to be postponed till the summer vacation, which was a long way off. In the meantime they spent their time hand in hand on the sidewalks or the forest paths (young lovers in those days were tireless walkers), sentenced to repetitive conversations and fondlings that led nowhere. There in that desert without ecstasy, he informed her that an unavoidable separation loomed, as he would soon be moving to Prague.

Josef is surprised to read this; moving to Prague? Such a plan was quite simply impossible, for his family had never had any intention of leaving their city. And suddenly the memory rises up out of oblivion, disagreeably present and vivid: he is standing on a forest path, in front of that girl, and he's talking to her about Prague! He is talking about moving away, and he's lying! He recalls perfectly his awareness of lying, he sees himself talking and lying, lying in order to see the high-school girl cry!

He reads: "Sobbing, she clasped me to her. I was extremely alert to every sign of her pain, and I regret that I no longer remember the exact number of her sobs."

Is this possible? "Extremely alert to every sign of her pain," he counted the sobs! That torturer-accountant! That was his way of feeling, of living, of savoring, of enacting love! He held her in his arms, she sobbed, and he counted!

He goes on reading: "Then she calmed down and told me: 'Now I understand those poets who stayed faithful unto death.' She looked up at me, and her lips *twitched*." The word "twitched" is underlined in the diary.

Josef recalls neither her words nor her twitching lips. The only vivid recollection is the moment when he was spouting those lies about moving to Prague. Nothing else remains in his memory. He strains to call up the features of that exotic girl who compared herself not to pop singers or tennis players but to poets, poets "who stayed faithful unto death"! He savors the anachronism of the carefully recorded expression, and feels more and more fondness for that girl, so sweetly old-fashioned. The one thing he holds against her is her having been in love with a detestable snot whose only desire was to torture her.

Oh, that snot! Josef can see him staring at the girl's lips, those twitching lips—uncontrolled, uncontrollable despite herself! He must have been aroused by the sight, as if he were watching an orgasm (a female orgasm, a thing he would have no idea of!) Maybe he got an erection! He must have!

Enough! Josef turns the pages and learns that the high-school girl was preparing to go off to the mountains for a week of skiing with her class; the little snot protested, threatened to break up with her; she told him the trip was a school requirement; he refused to listen and flew into a rage (another ecstasy! an ecstasy of rage!) "If you go, it's the end between us. I swear—the end!"

What did she answer? Did her lips twitch when she heard his hysterical outburst? Not likely, because that uncontrolled movement of the lips, that virginal orgasm, always aroused him so much that he would certainly have mentioned it. Apparently this time he overestimated his power. For there are no further references to his school-girl. There follow a few accounts of vapid dates with another girl (Josef skips over some lines),

86

and the diary finishes with the closing days of the school year (he has one more to go) just when an older woman (this one he remembers very well) introduced him to physical love and moved his life onto other tracks; he had stopped writing all that down by now; the diary did not outlive its author's virginity; a very brief chapter of his life came to an end, and, having neither sequel nor consequence, was relegated to the dim cupboard of cast-off items.

Josef sets about ripping the diary pages into tiny scraps. The gesture is probably excessive and useless; but he feels the need to give free rein to his aversion; the need to annihilate the little snot so that never (even if only in a bad dream) would he be mistaken for him, be vilified in his stead, be held responsible for his words and his acts!

25

At that moment the telephone rang. He remembered the woman from the Paris airport, and picked up the phone.

"You won't recognize me," said a voice.

"I do, sure I do!"

"But you can't know who you're talking to."

No, he was mistaken; it wasn't the woman from the airport. It was one of those blasé drawls, those unpleasantly nasal voices. He was disconcerted. She introduced herself: it was the daughter from her previous marriage of the woman he'd divorced after a few months of life together, thirty years back.

"No, you're right, I couldn't know who I was talking to," he said with a forced laugh.

Since the divorce he had never seen them, neither his ex-wife nor his stepdaughter, who in his memory was still a little girl.

"I need to talk to you," she said.

He regretted having begun the conversation so enthusiastically; he was unhappy with her tone of familiarity, but he couldn't do anything about that now: "How did you find out I was here? Nobody knows."

"Well, really."

"What do you mean?"

"Your sister-in-law."

"I didn't know you knew her."

"Mama does."

Immediately he pictured the alliance that had sprung up spontaneously between those two women.

"So then, you're calling on your mother's behalf?"

The blasé voice turned insistent. "I need to talk to you. It's absolutely necessary."

"You, or your mother?"

"Me."

"Tell me first what this is about."

"Do you want to see me or not?"

"I'm asking you to tell me what it's about."

The blasé voice turned aggressive: "If you don't want to see me, just say so right out."

He detested her insistence but did not dare put her off. Keeping secret her reason for the meeting was a very effective gambit on his stepdaughter's part: he grew uneasy.

"I'm only here for a couple of days; I'm very busy. I might be able to squeeze in a half hour at most . . . ," and he named a café in Prague for the day he was leaving.

"You won't be there."

"I'll be there."

When he hung up he felt a kind of nausea. What could those women want from him? Some advice? People who need advice don't act aggressive. They wanted to make trouble for him. Prove they existed. Take up his time. But then why had he agreed to meet her? Out of curiosity? Oh, come on—it was out of fear! He had given in to an old reflex: to protect himself he always tried to be fully informed in advance. But protect himself? These days? Against what? There was certainly no danger. Quite simply, his stepdaughter's voice enveloped him in a fog of old recollections: intrigues; interfering relatives; abortion; tears; slander; blackmail; emotional bullying; angry scenes; anonymous letters: the whole concierge conspiracy.

The life we've left behind us has a bad habit of stepping out of the shadows, of bringing complaints against us, of taking us to court. Living far from Bohemia, Josef had lost the habit of keeping his past in mind. But the past was there, waiting for him, watching him. Uneasy, Josef tried to think about other things. But when a man has come to look at the land of his past, what can he think about if not his past? In the two days left to him, what should he do? Pay a visit to the town where he'd had his veterinary practice? Go and stand, moist-eyed, before the house he used to live in? He hadn't the slightest desire to do that. Was there anyone at all among the people he used to know whom he would—sincerely—like to see? N.'s face emerged. Way back, when the rabble-rousers of the revolution accused the very young Josef of God knows what (in those years everyone, at some time or another, stood accused of God knows what), N., who was an influential Communist at the university, had stood up for him without worrying about Josef's opinions and family background. That was how they'd become friends, and if Josef could reproach himself for anything, it would be for having largely forgotten about the man during the twenty years since his emigration.

"The Red Commissar! Everyone was terrified of him!" his sister-in-law had said, implying that, out of self-interest, Josef had attached himself to a stalwart of the regime. Oh, those poor countries shaken by great historical dates! When the battle is over, everybody stampedes off on punitive expeditions into the past to hunt down the guilty parties. But who were the guilty parties? The

Communists who won in 1948? Or their ineffective adversaries who lost? Everybody was hunting down the guilty and everybody was being hunted down. When Josef's brother joined the Party so as to go on with his studies, his friends condemned him as an opportunist. That had made him detest Communism all the more, blaming it for his craven behavior, and his wife had focused her own hatred on people like N., who, as a convinced Marxist before the revolution, had of his own free will (and thus unpardonably) helped to bring about a system she held to be the greatest of all evils.

The telephone rang again. He picked it up, and this time he was sure he recognized her: "Finally!"

"Oh, I'm so glad to hear your 'finally!' Were you waiting for my call?"

"Impatiently."

"Really?"

"I was in a hideous mood! Hearing your voice changes everything!"

"Oh, you're making me very happy! How I wish you were with me—right here, where I am."

"How sorry I am that I can't be."

"You're sorry? Really?"

"Really."

"Will I see you before you leave?"

"Yes, you'll see me."

"For sure?"

"For sure! We'll have lunch together the day after tomorrow!"

"I'll be delighted."

He gave her the address of his hotel in Prague.

As he hung up, his glance fell on the shredded diary, now only a small pile of paper strips on the table. He picked up the whole bundle and merrily tossed it into the wastebasket.

26

Three years before 1989, Gustaf had opened an office in Prague for his company, but he only went there for a few visits each year. That was enough for him to love the city and to see it as an ideal place to live; not only out of love for Irena but also (maybe even especially) because there he felt, even more than in Paris, cut off from Sweden, from his family, from his past life. When Communism unexpectedly vanished from Europe, he was quick to tout Prague to his company as a strategic location for conquering new markets. He saw to the purchase of a handsome baroque house for office space, and set aside two rooms for himself up under the eaves. Meanwhile Irena's mother, who lived alone in a villa on the city's outskirts, put her whole second floor at Gustaf's disposal; he could thus switch living quarters as the mood struck him.

Sleepy and unkempt during the Communist period, Prague came awake before his eyes: it filled up with tourists, lit up with new shops and restaurants, dressed up with restored and repainted baroque houses. "Prague is my town!" he would exclaim in English. He was in love with the city: not like a patriot searching every corner of the land for his roots, his memories, the traces of his dead, but like a traveler responding with surprise and amazement, like a child wandering dazzled through an amusement park and reluctant ever to leave it. Having learned Prague's history, he would declaim at length to anyone who'd listen about its streets, its palaces, its churches, and hold forth endlessly on its stars: on Emperor Rudolf (protector of painters and alchemists), on Mozart (who, says the gossip, had a mistress there), on Franz Kafka (who though miserable throughout his lifetime in this city had, thanks to the travel agencies, turned into its patron saint).

At an unhoped-for speed Prague forgot the Russian language that for forty years all its inhabitants had been made to learn from grade school onward, and now, eager for applause on the world's proscenium, displayed to the visitors its new attire of English-language signs and labels. In Gustaf's company offices the staff, the trading associates, the rich customers all addressed him in English, so Czech was no more than an impersonal murmur, a background of sound against which only Anglo-American phonemes stood forth as human words. And one day when Irena landed in Prague, he greeted her at the airport not with their usual French "*Salut!*" but with a "Hello!"

Suddenly everything was different. For let's look at Irena's life after Martin died: she had nobody left to speak Czech with, her daughters refused to waste their time with such an obviously useless language; French was her everyday language, her only language, so it was quite natural for her to impose it on her Swede. This linguistic choice had determined their roles: since Gustaf spoke French poorly, it was she who led the talk within the couple; she grew giddy with her own eloquence: heavens, after so long she could finally speak, speak and be heard! Her verbal superiority balanced out their relative strengths: she was entirely dependent on him, but in their conversations she ruled, and she drew him into her own world.

Now Prague was reshaping their language as a couple; he spoke English, Irena tried to persist with her French, to which she felt ever more attached, but with no external support (French no longer held much charm for this previously Francophile city), she wound up capitulating; their interaction turned around: in Paris, Gustaf used to listen attentively to an Irena who thirsted for the sound of her own words; in Prague he turned into the talker, a big talker, a long talker. Knowing little English, Irena understood only half of what he said, and as she didn't feel like making much effort, she listened to him rather little and spoke to him still less. Her Great Return took a very odd twist: in the streets, surrounded by Czechs, the whiff of an old familiarity would caress her and for a moment make her happy; then, back in the house, she would become a silent foreigner.

Couples have a continuous conversation that lulls them, its melodious stream throwing a veil over the body's waning desires. When the conversation breaks off, the absence of physical love comes forward like a ghost. In the face of Irena's muteness, Gustaf lost his confidence. He came to prefer spending time with her in the presence of her family, her mother, her half-brother and his wife; he would dine with them all at the villa or at a restaurant, looking to their company for shelter, for refuge, for peace. They were never short of topics because they could only broach so few: their common vocabulary was limited, and to make themselves understood everyone had to speak slowly and keep repeating things. Gustaf was on the way to recovering his serenity; this slow-tempo babble suited him, it was restful, agreeable, and even merry (they were constantly laughing over their comical distortions of English words).

Irena's eyes were long since empty of desire, but from habit they still set their wide gaze on Gustaf and discomfited him. To cover his tracks and mask his erotic withdrawal, he took pleasure in good-naturedly dirty stories and mildly ambiguous allusions, all delivered loudly and with laughter. The mother was his best ally, ever quick to support him with smutty remarks that she would pronounce in some exaggerated, parodic manner, and in her puerile English. Listening to the two of them, Irena got the sense that eroticism had once and for all turned into childish clowning.

27

From the moment she ran into Josef at the Paris airport, she's been thinking of nothing but him. She constantly replays their brief encounter long ago in Prague. In the bar where she'd been sitting with friends, he was older and more interesting than the others, funny and seductive, and he paid attention only to her. When they had all gone out into the street, he saw to it that they were left to themselves. He slipped her a little ashtray he'd stolen for her from the bar. Then this man she had known for only a couple of hours invited her home with him. She was engaged to Martin, and she couldn't work up the nerve; she'd refused. But immediately she had felt such an abrupt, piercing regret that she has never forgotten it.

And so, when she was preparing to emigrate, sorting out what to take with her and what to leave behind, she had stuck the little ashtray into a valise; abroad, she often carried it in her purse, secretly, like a good luck charm.

She recalls that in the airport lounge he had said in a grave, strange tone: "I'm a completely free man." She had the sense that their love story, begun twenty years earlier, had merely been postponed until the two of them should be free.

And she recalls another of his remarks: "It's pure chance that I'm going through Paris"; "chance" is another way of saying "fate"; he had to go through Paris so that their story could take up at the point where it had been interrupted.

With her cell phone in hand, she tries to reach him from wherever she is—cafés, a friend's apartment, the street. The hotel number is correct, but he's never in his room. All day long she thinks about him and, since opposites attract, about Gustaf. Passing a souvenir shop, she sees in the window a T-shirt showing the gloomy face of a tubercular, with a line in English: KAFKA WAS BORN IN PRAGUE. A magnificently stupid T-shirt, it enchants her, and she buys it.

Toward evening she returns to the house meaning to phone him undisturbed from there, because on Fridays Gustaf always comes home late; against all expectations he is on the ground floor with her mother, and the room resounds with their Czech-English babble over the voice of a television anchorman no one is watching. She hands Gustaf a little package: "For you!"

Then she leaves them to admire the gift and goes up to their rooms on the second floor, where she shuts herself into the bathroom. Sitting on the rim of the toilet, she pulls the telephone out of her purse. She hears his "Finally!" and, overcome with joy, tells him, "Oh, how I wish you were with me—right here, where I am"; only after she speaks those words does she realize where she's sitting, and she blushes; the unintended indecency of what she's said startles her and instantly arouses her. At that moment, for the first time after so many years, she has the sense that she's cheating on her Swede, and takes a vicious pleasure in it.

When she goes back down to the living room, Gustaf is wearing the T-shirt and laughing raucously. She knows the scene by heart: parody seduction, overbroad witticisms: a senile counterfeit of burned-out eroticism. The mother is holding Gustaf's hand and she announces to Irena: "Without your permission I went ahead and dressed up your boyfriend. Isn't he gorgeous?" She turns with him toward a great mirror hanging on the wall. Watching their reflection, she raises Gustaf's arm as if he were a winner at the Olympics, and, going along with the game, he swells his chest for the mirror and declares in ringing tones: "Kafka was born in Prague!"

She had separated from her first boyfriend with no great pain. With the second it was worse. When she heard him say, "If you go, it's the end between us. I swear—the end!" she could not utter a single word. She loved him, and he was flinging in her face a thing that, only a few minutes earlier, she would have thought inconceivable, unspeakable: their breakup.

"It's the end between us." The end. If he's promising her the end, what should she promise him? His words contain a threat; so will hers: "All right," she says slowly and evenly. "Then it will be the end. I promise you that, too, and you won't forget it." Then she turned her back on him, leaving him standing right there in the street.

She was wounded, but was she angry with him? Perhaps not even. Of course, he ought to have been more understanding, for clearly she could not pull out of the trip, which was a school requirement. She would have had to feign an illness, but with her clumsy honesty, she could never have pulled it off. No question, he was overdoing it, he was unfair, but she knew it was because he loved her. She understood his jealousy: he was imagining her off in the mountains with other boys, and it upset him.

Incapable of real anger, she waited for him outside school, to explain that with the best will in the world, she really couldn't do what he wanted, and that he had no reason to be jealous; she was sure he would understand. From the doorway he saw her and dropped back to fall into step with a friend. Denied a private conversation, she followed behind him through the streets, and when he took leave of the friend she hurried toward him. Poor thing, she should have suspected that there wasn't a chance, that her sweetheart was caught up in an unremitting frenzy. She had barely begun to speak when he broke in: "You've changed your mind? You're cancelling?" When she started to say the same thing again for the tenth time, he was the one who spun on his heel and left her standing alone in the middle of the street.

She fell back into a deep sorrow, but still without anger at him. She knew that love means giving each other everything. "Everything": that word is fundamental. Everything, thus not only the physical love she had promised him, but courage too, the courage for big things as well as small ones, which is to say even the puny courage to disobey a silly school requirement. And in shame she saw that despite all her love, she was not capable of mustering that courage. It was grotesque, heartbreakingly grotesque: here she was prepared to give him everything, her virginity of course, but also, if he wanted it, her health and any sacrifice he could think up, and still she couldn't bring herself to disobey a miserable school principal. Should she let herself be defeated by such pettiness? Her self-disgust was unbearable, and she wanted to get free of it at any cost; she wanted to reach some greatness in which her pettiness would disappear; a greatness before which he would ultimately have to bow down; she wanted to die.

29

To die; to decide to die; that's much easier for an adolescent than for an adult. What? Doesn't death strip an adolescent of a far larger portion of future? Certainly it does, but for a young person, the future is a remote, abstract, unreal thing he doesn't really believe in.

Transfixed, she watched her shattered love, the most beautiful piece of her life, drawing away slowly and forever; nothing existed for her except that past; to it she wanted to make herself known, wanted to speak and send signals. The future held no interest for her; she desired eternity; eternity is time that has stopped, come to a standstill; the future makes eternity impossible; she wanted to annihilate the future.

But how can a person die in the midst of a crowd of students, in a little mountain hotel, constantly in plain view? She figured it out: she'll leave the hotel, walk far, very far, into the wild, and, someplace off the trails, lie down in the snow and go to sleep. Death will come during slumber, death by freezing, a sweet, painless death. She will only have to get through a brief stretch of cold. And even that, she can shorten with the help of a few sleeping tablets. From a vial unearthed at home she poured out five of them, no more, so Mama wouldn't miss them.

She laid plans for her death with her usual practicality. Her first idea was to leave the hotel late in the day and die at night, but she dropped that: people would be quick to miss her in the dining room and even more surely in the dormitory; she wouldn't have time enough to die. Cunningly she decided on the hour after lunch, when everyone naps before heading back to ski: a recess when her absence would worry nobody.

Could she not see a blatant disproportion between the triviality of the cause and the hugeness of the act? Did she not know that her project was excessive? Of course she did, but the excess was precisely what appealed to her. She did not want to be reasonable. She did not want to behave in a measured way. She did not want to measure, she did not want to reason. She admired her passion, knowing that passion is by definition excessive. Intoxicated, she did not want to emerge from intoxication.

Then comes the appointed day. She leaves the hotel. Beside the door hangs a thermometer: minus ten degrees Celsius. She sets out and realizes that her intoxicated state has been succeeded by anxiety; in vain she seeks her previous enthrallment, in vain she calls for the ideas that had surrounded her dream of death; in vain, but nonetheless she keeps walking the trail (her schoolmates are meanwhile taking their required siestas) as if she were performing a chore she'd set herself, as if she were playing a role she'd assigned herself. Her soul is empty, without emotion, like the soul of an actor reciting a text and no longer thinking about what he's saying.

She climbs a trail glistening with snow and soon reaches the crest. The sky above is blue; the many clouds—sun-drenched, gilded, lively—have moved down, settled like a great diadem on the broad ring of the encircling mountains. It is beautiful, it is mesmerizing, and she has a brief, very brief, sensation of happiness, which makes her forget the purpose of her walk. A brief, very brief, too brief sensation. One after the other she swallows the tablets and, following her plan, walks down from the crest into a forest. She steps along a footpath; in ten minutes she feels sleep coming on, and she knows the end has come. The sun is overhead, brilliant, brilliant. As if the curtain were suddenly lifting, her heart tightens with stagefright. She feels trapped on a lighted stage with all the exits blocked.

She sits down beneath a fir tree, opens her bag, and takes out a mirror. It is a small round mirror; she holds it up to her face and looks at herself. She is beautiful, she is very beautiful, and she does not want to part from this beauty, she does not want to lose it, she wants to carry it away with her, ah, she is already weary, so weary, but even weary she rejoices in her beauty because it is what she cherishes most in this world.

She looks in the mirror, then she sees her lips twitch. It is an involuntary movement, a tic. She has often registered that reaction of hers, she has felt it happening on her face, but this is the first time she is seeing it. At the sight she is doubly moved: moved by her beauty and moved by her lips twitching; moved by her beauty and moved by the emotion wracking that beauty and distorting it; moved by her beauty that her body laments. An enormous pity overtakes her, pity for

108

her beauty that will soon cease to be, pity for the world that will also cease to be, that already does not exist, that is already out of reach, for sleep has come, it is carrying her away, flying off with her, high up, very high, toward that enormous blinding brilliance, toward the blue, brilliantly blue sky, a cloudless firmament, a firmament ablaze.

30

When his brother said, "You got married over there, I believe," he answered "Yes" with no further remark. His brother might merely have used some other turn of phrase, and rather than saying, "You got married," asked, "Are you married?" In that case Josef would have answered, "No, widowed." He hadn't meant to mislead his brother, but the way the query was phrased allowed him, without lying, to keep silent about his wife's death.

During the conversation that followed, his brother and sister-in-law avoided any mention of her. That must have been out of embarrassment:

for security reasons (to avoid being questioned by the police) they had denied themselves the slightest contact with their émigré relative and never even realized that their forced caution had soon turned into authentic lack of interest: they knew nothing about his wife, not her age or her given name or her profession, and by keeping their silence now they hoped to disguise that ignorance, which showed up the terrible poverty of their relations with him.

But Josef took no offense; their ignorance suited him fine. Since the day he buried her, he had always felt uncomfortable when he had to inform someone of her death; as if by doing so he were betraying her in her most private privacy. By not speaking of her death, he always felt he was protecting her.

For the woman who is dead is a woman with no defenses; she has no more power, she has no more influence; people no longer respect either her wishes or her tastes; the dead woman cannot will anything, cannot aspire to any respect or refute any slander. Never had he felt such sorrowful, such agonizing compassion for her as when she was dead.

31

Jonas Hallgrimsson was a great romantic poet and also a great fighter for Iceland's independence. In the nineteenth century all of small-nation Europe had these romantic patriot-poets: Petöfi in Hungary, Mickiewicz in Poland, Preseren in Slovenia, Macha in Bohemia, Shevchenko in Ukraine, Wergeland in Norway, Lönnrot in Finland, and the like. Iceland was a colony of Denmark at the time, and Hallgrimsson lived out his last years in the Danish capital. All the great romantic poets, besides being great patriots, were great drinkers. One day, dead drunk, Hallgrimsson fell down a staircase, broke a leg, got an infection, died, and was buried in a Copenhagen cemetery. That was in 1845. Ninety-nine years later, in 1944, the Icelandic Republic declared its independence. From then on events hastened their course. In 1946 the poet's soul visited a rich Icelandic industrialist in his sleep and confided: "For a hundred years now my skeleton has lain in a foreign land, in the enemy country. Is it not time it came home to its own free Ithaca?"

Flattered and elated by this nocturnal visit, the patriotic industrialist had the poet's skeleton dug out of the enemy soil and carried back to Iceland, intending to bury it in the lovely valley where the poet had been born. But no one can stop the mad course of events: in the ineffably exquisite landscape of Thingvellir (the sacred place where, a thousand years ago, the first Icelandic parliament gathered beneath the open sky), the ministers of the brand-new republic had created a cemetery for the great men of the homeland; they ripped the poet away from the industrialist and buried him in the pantheon that at the time contained only the grave of another great poet (small nations abound in great poets), Einar Benediktsson.

But again events rushed on, and soon everyone learned what the patriotic industrialist had never dared admit: standing at the opened tomb back in Copenhagen, he had felt extremely disconcerted: the poet had been buried in a paupers' field with no name marking his grave, only a number and, confronted with a bunch of skeletons tangled together, the patriotic industrialist had not known which one to pick. In the presence of the stern, impatient cemetery bureaucrats, he did not dare show his uncertainty. And so he had transported to Iceland not the Icelandic poet but a Danish butcher.

In Iceland people had initially tried to hush up this lugubriously comical mistake, but events continued to run their course, and in 1948 the indiscreet writer Halldor Laxness spilled the beans in a novel. What to do? Keep quiet. Therefore Hallgrimsson's bones still lie two thousand miles away from his Ithaca, in enemy soil, while the body of the Danish butcher, who although no poet was a patriot as well, still lies banished to a glacial island that never stirred him to anything but fear and repugnance.

Even hushed up, the consequence of the truth was that no one else was ever buried in the exquisite cemetery at Thingvellir, which harbors only two coffins and which thereby, of all the world's pantheons, those grotesque museums of pride, is the only one capable of touching our hearts.

A very long time ago Josef's wife had told him that story; they thought it was funny, and a moral lesson seemed easily drawn from it: nobody much cares where a dead person's bones wind up.

And yet Josef changed his mind when his wife's

death became imminent and inevitable. Suddenly the story of the Danish butcher abducted to Iceland seemed not funny but terrifying.

32

The idea of dying when she did had been with him for a long time. It was due not to romantic grandiosity but rather to a rational consideration: if ever his wife should be struck by a fatal illness, he had determined he would cut short her suffering; to avoid being indicted for murder, he planned to die as well. Then she actually did fall gravely ill, and suffered terribly, and Josef no longer had a mind for suicide. Not out of fear for his own life. But he found intolerable the idea of leaving that very beloved body to the mercy of alien hands. With him dead, who would protect the dead woman? How could one corpse keep another one safe?

Long ago in Bohemia, he had watched over his mother's dying agony; he loved her very much, but once she was no longer alive, her body ceased to interest him; to his mind her corpse was no longer she. Besides, two doctors, his father and his brother, took care of the dying woman, and in the order of importance he was just the third family member. This time everything was different: the woman he saw dying belonged to him alone; he was jealous for her body and wanted to watch over its posthumous fate. He even had to admonish himself: here she was still alive, lying in front of him, she was speaking to him, and he was already thinking of her as dead; she was gazing up at him, her eyes larger than ever, and his mind was busy with her casket and her grave. He scolded himself for that as if it were a shocking betrayal, an impatience, a secret wish to hasten her death. But he couldn't help it: he knew that after the death, her family would come to claim her for their family vault, and the idea horrified him.

Contemptuous of funeral concerns, in writing their wills sometime earlier he and she had been too offhand; their instructions on disposing of their possessions were very rudimentary, and they hadn't even mentioned burial. The omission obsessed him while she was dying, but since he was trying to convince her that she would beat death, he had to hold his tongue. How could he confess to the poor woman who still believed she would recover, how could he confess what he was thinking about? How could he talk about the will? Especially since she was already slipping into spells of delirium, and her thinking was muddled.

His wife's family, a prominent and influential family, had never liked Josef. It seemed to him that the struggle ahead for his wife's body would be the toughest and most important he would ever fight. The idea that this body would be locked into an obscene promiscuity with other bodies, unknown and meaningless, was unbearable to him, as was the idea that he himself, when he died, would end up who knew where and certainly far away from her. To let that happen seemed a defeat as huge as eternity, a defeat never to be forgiven.

What he feared came about. He could not avoid the shock. His mother-in-law railed against him: "It's my daughter! It's my daughter!" He had to hire a lawyer, hand over a bundle of money to pacify the family, hastily buy a cemetery plot, act more quickly than the others to win this final combat.

The feverish activity of a sleepless week fended off his suffering, but something even stranger occurred: when she was in the grave that belonged to them (a grave for two, like a two-seat buggy), in the darkness of his sorrow he glimpsed a feeble, trembling, barely visible ray of happiness. Happiness at not having let down his beloved; at having provided for their future, his and hers both.

33

An instant earlier she had been drenched in the radiant blue! She was immaterial, transmuted into brilliance!

And then, abruptly, the sky went black. And she, fallen back onto the earth, turned into heavy dark matter. Scarcely understanding what had happened, she could not tear her gaze away from up there: the sky was black, black, implacably black.

One part of her body chattered with cold, the other was numb. That frightened her. She stood up. After several long moments she remembered: a hotel in the mountains; classmates. Dazed, her body shaking, she looked for the path. At the hotel they called an ambulance, and it took her away.

Over the next days in her hospital bed, her fingers, her ears, her nose, which at first were numb, gave her terrific pain. The doctors reassured her, but one nurse took delight in reciting all the conceivable effects of freezings: a person could end up with his fingers amputated. Stricken with terror, she imagined an ax; a surgeon's ax; a butcher's ax; she imagined her fingerless hand and its severed fingers lying beside her on an operating table, for her to see. At night, for supper, they brought her meat. She could not eat. She imagined chunks of her own flesh on the plate.

Her fingers came painfully back to life, but her left ear turned black. The surgeon, an elderly, sorrowful, compassionate man, sat on her bed to tell her it must be amputated. She screamed. Her left ear! My God, how she screamed! Her face, her lovely face, with an ear cut off! No one could calm her.

118

Oh, everything had gone the opposite of what she'd intended! She had meant to become an eternity that would abolish the whole future, and instead, the future was back again, invincible, hideous, repugnant, like a snake writhing in front of her and rubbing against her legs and slithering ahead to show her the way.

At school the news spread that she had got lost and had come back covered with frostbite. People blamed her as a headstrong girl who skipped the required program and went wandering stupidly off with not even an elementary sense of direction for finding her way back to the hotel, which could actually be seen from a distance.

Home from the hospital, she refused to go outdoors. She was terrified of running into people she knew. In despair her parents arranged a quiet transfer to another high school, in a nearby town.

Oh, everything had gone the opposite of what she'd intended! She had dreamed of dying mysteriously. She had done her best so no one could tell whether her death was an accident or a suicide. She had meant to send him her death as a secret sign, a sign of love transmitted from the beyond, comprehensible to no one but him. She had anticipated everything except, perhaps, the number of sleeping tablets; except, perhaps, the temperature, which as she was drowsing off had gone up. She had expected that the freeze would plunge her into sleep and into death, but the sleep was too weak; she had opened her eyes and seen the black sky.

Those two skies had divided her life into two parts: blue sky, black sky. The second sky was the one she would walk beneath to her death, her true death, the faraway and trivial death of old age.

And he? He was living beneath a sky that had nothing to do with her. He no longer sought her out, she no longer sought him out. Recalling him awakened neither love nor hatred in her. At the thought of him, she was as if anesthetized—with no ideas, no emotions.

34

A human lifetime is 80 years long on average. A person imagines and organizes his life with that span in mind. What I have just said everyone knows, but only rarely do we realize that the number of years granted us is not merely a quantitative fact, an external feature (like nose length or eye color), but is part of the very definition of the human. A person who might live, with all his faculties, twice as long, say 160 years, would not belong to our species. Nothing about his life would be like ours—not love, or ambitions, or feelings, or nostalgia; nothing. If after 20 years abroad an émigré were to come back to his native land with another hundred years of life ahead of him, he would have little sense of a Great Return, for him it would probably not be a return at all, just one of many byways in the long journey of his life.

For the very notion of homeland, with all its emotional power, is bound up with the relative brevity of our life, which allows us too little time to become attached to some other country, to other countries, to other languages.

Sexual relations can take up the whole of adult life. But if that life were a lot longer, might not staleness stifle the capacity for arousal well before one's physical powers declined? For there is an enormous difference between the first and the tenth, the hundredth, the thousandth, or the ten-thousandth coitus. Where lies the boundary line beyond which repetition becomes stereotyped, if not comical or even impossible? And once that boundary is crossed, what would become of the erotic relationship between a man and a woman? Would it vanish? Or, on the contrary, would lovers consider the sexual phase of their lives to be the barbaric prehistory of real love? Answering these questions is as easy as imagining the psychology of the inhabitants of an unknown planet.

The notion of love (of great love, of one-and-only love) itself also derives, probably, from the narrow bounds of the time we are granted. If that time were boundless, would Josef be so attached to his deceased wife? We who must die so soon, we just don't know.

35

Memory cannot be understood, either, without a mathematical approach. The fundamental given is the ratio between the amount of time in the lived life and the amount of time from that life that is stored in memory. No one has ever tried to calculate this ratio, and in fact there exists no technique for doing so; yet without much risk of error I could assume that the memory retains no more than a millionth, a hundred-millionth, in short an utterly infinitesimal bit of the lived life. That fact too is part of the essence of man. If someone could retain in his memory everything he had experienced, if he could at any time call up any fragment of his past, he would be nothing like human beings: neither his loves nor his friendships nor his angers nor his capacity to forgive or avenge would resemble ours.

We will never cease our critique of those persons who distort the past, rewrite it, falsify it, who exaggerate the importance of one event and fail to mention some other; such a critique is proper (it cannot fail to be), but it doesn't count for much unless a more basic critique precedes it: a critique of human memory as such. For after all, what can memory actually do, the poor thing? It is only capable of retaining a paltry little scrap of the past, and no one knows why just this scrap and not some other one, since in each of us the choice occurs mysteriously, outside our will or our interests. We won't understand a thing about human life if we persist in avoiding the most obvious fact: that a reality no longer is what it was when it was; it cannot be reconstructed.

Even the most voluminous archives cannot help. Consider Josef's old diary as an archival document that preserves notes by the authentic witness to a certain past; the notes speak of events that their author has no reason to repudiate but that his memory cannot confirm, either. Out of everything the diary describes, only one detail sparked a clear, and certainly accurate, memory: he saw himself on a forest path telling a high-school girl the lie about his moving to Prague; that little scene, or more precisely that shadow of a scene (for he recalls only the general tenor of his remark and the fact of having lied), is the sole scrap of life that is still stored away, asleep, in his memory. But it is isolated from what preceded it and what followed it: by what remark, what action of her own had the high-school girl incited him to invent that phony story? And what happened in the days after that? How long did he keep up his deception? And how did he get out of it?

If he should want to recount that recollection as a little anecdote that made sense, he would have to insert it into a causal sequence with other events, other acts, and other words; and since he has forgotten them, all he could do was invent them; not to fool anyone but to make the recollection intelligible; which is exactly what he did automatically for his own sake when he rethought that passage in the diary:

The little snot was in despair at finding no sign of ecstasy in the love of his high-school girl; when he touched her rump, she lifted his hand away; to punish her he told her that he would be moving to Prague; pained, she let him pet her and declared that she understood the poets who stayed faithful unto death; so everything turned out blissfully for him, except that after a week or two the girl deduced from her boyfriend's plans to move that she ought to replace him soon with someone else; she began looking around; the little snot got wind of it and was uncontrollably jealous; taking as pretext a school excursion she was required to join without him, he threw a tantrum; he made a fool of himself; she dropped him.

Although he meant to get as close as possible to

the truth, Josef could not claim that his anecdote was identical with what he had actually experienced; he knew that it was only the plausible plastered over the forgotten.

I imagine the feelings of two people meeting again after many years. In the past they spent some time together, and therefore they think they are linked by the same experience, the same recollections. The same recollections? That's where the misunderstanding starts: they don't have the same recollections; each of them retains two or three small scenes from the past, but each has his own; their recollections are not similar; they don't intersect; and even in terms of quantity they are not comparable: one person remembers the other more than he is remembered; first because memory capacity varies among individuals (an explanation that each of them would at least find acceptable), but also (and this is more painful to admit) because they don't hold the same importance for each other. When Irena saw Josef at the airport, she remembered every detail of their long-ago adventure; Josef remembered nothing. From the very first moment their encounter was based on an unjust and revolting inequality.

36

When two people live in the same apartment, see each other every day, and also love each other, their daily conversations bring their two memories into line: by tacit and unconscious consent they leave vast areas of their life unremembered, and they talk time and time again about the same few events out of which they weave a joint narrative that, like a breeze in the boughs, murmurs above their heads and reminds them constantly that they have lived together.

When Martin died, the violent current of worries carried Irena far away from him and from the people who knew him. He vanished from conversations, and even his two daughters, who were too young when he was alive, took no further interest in him. One day she met Gustaf, and to prolong their conversation, he told her he had known her husband. That was the last time that Martin was with her, a strong, important, influential presence serving as a bridge to the man who was soon to be her lover. Once Martin had fulfilled that mission, he withdrew for good.

Long before, in Prague, on their wedding day, Martin had settled Irena in his villa; his own library and office were on the second floor, and he kept the street level for his life as husband and father; before they left for France he transferred the villa to his mother-in-law, and twenty years later she gave Gustaf that second floor, by then entirely refurbished. When Milada came there to visit Irena, she reminisced about her former colleague: "This is where Martin used to work," she said, reflective. But no shade of Martin appeared after those words. He had long ago been dislodged from the house, he and all his shades.

After his wife's death Josef noticed that without daily conversations, the murmur of their past life grew faint. To intensify it, he tried to revive his wife's image, but the lackluster result distressed him. She'd had a dozen different smiles. He strained his imagination to re-create them. He failed. She'd had a gift for fast funny lines that would delight him. He couldn't call forth a single one. He finally wondered: if he were to add up the few recollections he still had from their life together, how much time would they take? A minute? Two minutes?

That's another enigma about memory, more basic than all the rest: do recollections have some measurable temporal volume? do they unfold over a span of time? He tries to picture their first encounter: he sees a staircase leading down from the sidewalk into a beer cellar; he sees couples here and there in a yellow half-light; and he sees her, his future wife, sitting across from him, a brandy glass in hand, her gaze fixed on him, with a shy smile. For a long while he watches her holding her glass and smiling; he scrutinizes this face, this hand, and through all this time she remains motionless, does not lift the glass to her mouth or change her smile in the slightest. And there lies the horror: the past we remember is devoid of time. Impossible to reexperience a love the way we reread a book or resee a film. Dead, Josef's wife has no dimension at all, either material or temporal.

Therefore all efforts to revive her in his mind soon became torture. Instead of rejoicing at having retrieved this or that forgotten moment, he was driven to despair by the immensity of the void around that moment. Then one day he forbade himself that painful ramble through the corridors of the past, and stopped his vain efforts to bring her back as she had been. He even thought that by his fixation on her bygone existence, he was traitorously relegating her to a museum of vanished objects and excluding her from his present life.

Besides, they had never made a cult of reminiscence. Not that they'd destroyed their private correspondence, of course, or their datebooks with notes on errands and appointments. But it never occurred to them to reread them. He therefore determined to live with the dead woman the way he had with the living one. He now went to her grave not to reminisce but to spend time with her; to see her eyes looking at him, and looking not from the past but from the present moment.

And now a new life began for him: living with the dead woman. There is a new clock organizing his time. A stickler for tidiness, she used to be irritated by the disorder he left everywhere. Now he does the housecleaning himself, meticulously. For he loves their home even more now than he did when she was alive: the low wooden fence with its little gate; the garden; the fir tree in front of the dark-red brick house; the two facing easy chairs they'd sit in at the end of the working day; the window ledge where she always kept a bowl of flowers on one end, a lamp on the other; they would leave that lamp on while they were out so they could see it from afar as they came down the street back to the house. He respects all those customs, and he takes care to see that every chair, every vase is where she liked to have it.

He revisits the places they loved: the seaside restaurant where the owner invariably reminds him of his wife's favorite fish dishes; in a small town nearby, the rectangle of the town square with red-, blue-, yellow-painted houses, a modest beauty they found enthralling; or, on a visit to Copenhagen, the wharf where every evening at six a great white steamship set out to sea. There they could stand motionless for a long time watching it. Before it sailed music would ring out, old-time jazz, the invitation to the voyage. Since her death he often goes there; he imagines her beside him and feels again their mutual yearning to climb aboard that white nocturnal ship, to dance on it and sleep on it and wake up somewhere far, very far, to the north.

She liked him to dress well, and she saw to his

wardrobe herself. He hasn't forgotten which of his shirts she liked and which she did not. For this visit to Bohemia, he purposely packed a suit she'd had no feeling for either way. He did not want to grant this journey too much attention. It is not a journey for her, or with her.

37

Completely focused on her next-day's rendezvous, Irena means to spend this Saturday in peace and quiet, like an athlete on the eve of a match. Gustaf is working in the city, and he'll be out for the evening as well. She takes advantage of her solitude, she sleeps late and then stays in their rooms, trying not to run into her mother; downstairs she can hear the woman's comings and goings, which end only around noon. When finally she hears the door slam hard and is sure her mother has left the house, she goes down to the kitchen, absentmindedly eats a little something, and takes off as well.

On the sidewalk she stops, enthralled. In the

autumn sunshine this garden neighborhood scattered with little villas reveals a quiet beauty that grips her heart and lures her into a long walk. It reminds her that she had wanted to take just such a walk, long and contemplative, in the last days before her emigration, so as to bid farewell to this city, to all the streets she had loved; but there were too many things to arrange, and she never found the time.

Seen from where she is strolling, Prague is a broad green swath of peaceable neighborhoods with narrow tree-lined streets. This is the Prague she loves, not the sumptuous one downtown; the Prague born at the turn of the previous century, the Prague of the Czech lower middle class, the Prague of her childhood, where in wintertime she would ski up and down the hilly little lanes, the Prague where at dusk the encircling forests would steal into town to spread their fragrance.

Dreamily she walks on; for a few seconds she catches a glimpse of Paris, which for the first time she feels has something hostile about it: chilly geometry of the avenues; pridefulness of the Champs-Elysées; stern countenances of the giant stone women representing Equality or Fraternity;

and nowhere, nowhere, a single touch of this kindly intimacy, a single whiff of this idyll she inhales here. In fact, throughout all her years as an émigré, this is the picture she has harbored as the emblem of her lost country: little houses in gardens stretching away out of sight over rolling land. She felt happy in Paris, happier than here, but only Prague held her by a secret bond of beauty. She suddenly understands how much she loves this city and how painful her departure from it must have been.

She recalls those final feverish days: in the confusion of the early months of the Russian occupation, leaving the country was still easy to do, and they could say goodbye to their friends without fear. But they had too little time to see all of them. On a momentary impulse, two days before they left they went to visit an old friend, a bachelor, and spent some emotional hours with him. Only later, in France, did they learn that the reason this man had been so attentive to them over time was that the police had selected him to inform on Martin. The day before they left, she rang a friend's doorbell without having phoned ahead. She found her in a deep discussion with another woman. Saying nothing herself, she listened for a long time to a conversation of no concern to her, waiting for some gesture, an encouraging word, a goodbye; in vain. Had they forgotten she was leaving? Or were they pretending to forget? Or was it that neither her presence nor her absence mattered to them anymore? And her mother. As they were leaving, she did not kiss Irena. She kissed Martin, but not her. Irena she squeezed hard on the shoulder as she uttered in her resonant voice: "We don't go in for displaying our feelings!" The words were supposed to sound gruff and manly, but they were chilling. Remembering now all those farewells (fake farewells, worked-up farewells), Irena thinks: a person who messes up her goodbyes shouldn't expect much from her reunions.

By now she's been walking for a good two or three hours in those leafy neighborhoods. She reaches a parapet at the end of a little park above Prague: the view from here is of the rear of Hradcany Castle, the secret side; this is a Prague whose existence Gustaf doesn't suspect; and instantly there come rushing the names she loved as a young girl: Macha, poet at the time when his nation, a water sprite, was just emerging from the mists; Jan Neruda, the storyteller of ordinary Czech folk; the songs of Voskovec and Werich from the 1930s, so loved by her father, who died when she was a child; Hrabal and Skvorecky, novelists of her adolescence; and the little theaters and cabarets of the sixties, so free, so merrily free, with their sassy humor; it was the incommunicable scent of this country, its intangible essence, that she had brought along with her to France.

Leaning on the parapet, she looks over at the Castle: it's no more than fifteen minutes away. The Prague of the postcards begins there, the Prague that a frenzied history stamped with its multiple stigmata, the Prague of tourists and whores, the Prague of restaurants so expensive that her Czech friends can't set foot in them, the belly-dancer Prague writhing in the spotlight, Gustaf's Prague. She reflects that there is no place more alien to her than that Prague. Gustaftown. Gustafville. Gustafstadt. Gustafgrad.

Gustaf: she sees him, his features blurred through the clouded windowpane of a language she barely knows, and she thinks, almost joyfully, that it's fine this way because the truth is finally revealed: she feels no need to understand him or to have him understand her. She pictures his jovial figure, dressed up in his T-shirt, shouting that Kafka was born in Prague, and she feels a desire rising through her body, the irrepressible desire to take a lover. Not to patch up her life as it is. But to turn it completely upside down. Finally take possession of her own fate.

For she has never chosen any of her men. She was always the one being chosen. Martin she came to love, but at the start he was just a way to escape her mother. In her liaison with Gustaf she thought she was gaining freedom. But now she sees that it was only a variant of her relation with Martin: she seized an outstretched hand, and it pulled her out of difficult circumstances that she was unable to handle.

She knows she is good at gratitude; she has always prided herself on that as her prime virtue; when gratitude required it, a feeling of love would come running like a docile servant. She was sincerely devoted to Martin; she was sincerely devoted to Gustaf. But was that something to be proud of? Isn't gratitude simply another name for weakness, for dependency? What she wants now is love with no gratitude to it at all! And she knows that a love like that has to be bought by some daring, risky act. For she has never been daring in her love life, she didn't even know what that meant.

Suddenly, like a gust of wind: the high-speed parade of old emigration-dreams, old anxieties: she sees women rush up, surround her and, waving beer mugs and laughing falsely, keep her from escaping; she is in a shop where other women, salesgirls, dart over to her, put her into a dress that, once on her body, turns into a straitjacket.

For another long while she goes on leaning on the parapet, then she straightens up. She is suffused with the certainty that she will escape; that she will not stay on in this city; neither in this city nor in the life this city is weaving for her.

She moves on, and she reflects that today she is finally carrying out the farewell walk she failed to take last time; she is finally saying her Great Farewells to the city that she loves more than any other and that she is prepared to lose once again, without regret, to be worthy of a life of her own.

38

When Communism departed from Europe, Josef's wife kept pressing him to go see his country again. She intended to go with him. But she died, and from then on all he could think about was his new life with the absent woman. He tried hard to persuade himself that it was a happy life. But is "happiness" the right word? Yes; happiness like a frail, tremulous ray gleaming through his grief, a resigned, calm, unremitting grief. A month earlier, unable to shake the sadness, he recalled the words of his deceased wife: "Not going would be unnatural of you, unjustifiable, even foul"; actually, he thought, this trip she had so urged on him might possibly be some help to him now; might divert him, for a few days at least, from his own life, which was giving him such pain.

As he prepared for the trip, an idea tentatively crossed his mind: what if he were to stay over there for good? After all, he could be a veterinarian as easily in Bohemia as in Denmark. Till then the idea had seemed unacceptable, almost like a betrayal of the woman he loved. But he wondered:

would it really be a betrayal? If his wife's presence is nonmaterial, why should she be bound to the materiality of one particular place? Couldn't she be with him in Bohemia just as well as in Denmark?

He has left the hotel and is driving around in the car; he has lunch in a country inn; then he takes a walk through the fields; narrow lanes, wild roses, trees, trees; oddly moved, he gazes at the wooded hills on the horizon, and it occurs to him that twice in his own lifetime, the Czechs were willing to die to keep that landscape their own; in 1938 they wanted to fight Hitler; when their allies, the French and the English, kept them from doing so, they were in despair. In 1968 the Russians invaded the country, and again they wanted to fight; condemned to the same capitulation, they fell back into that same despair again.

To be willing to die for one's country: every nation has known that temptation to sacrifice. Indeed, the Czechs' adversaries also knew it: the Germans, the Russians. But those are large nations. Their patriotism is different: they are buoyed by their glory, their importance, their universal mission. The Czechs loved their country not because it was glorious but because it was unknown; not because it was big but because it was small and in constant danger. Their patriotism was an enormous compassion for their country. The Danes are like that too. Not by chance did Josef choose a small country for his emigration.

Much moved, he gazes out over the landscape and reflects that the history of his Bohemia during this past half century is fascinating, unique, unprecedented, and that failing to take an interest in it would be narrowminded. Tomorrow morning, he'll be seeing N. What kind of life did the man have during all the time they were out of touch? What had he thought about the Russian occupation of the country? And what was it like for him to see the end of the Communism he used to believe in, sincerely and honorably? How is his Marxist background adjusting to the return of this capitalism that's being cheered along by the entire planet? Is he rebelling against it? Or has he abandoned his convictions? And if he's abandoned them, is that a crisis for him? And how are other people behaving toward him? Josef can hear the voice of his sister-in-law who, huntress of the guilty, would certainly like to see N. handcuffed in court. Doesn't N. need Josef to tell him that friendship does exist despite all of history's contortions?

Josef's thoughts return to his sister-in-law: she hated the Communists because they disputed the sacred right of property. And then, he thought, she disputes my sacred right to my painting. He imagines the painting on a wall in his brick house in Copenhagen, and suddenly, with surprise, he realizes that the working-class suburb in the picture, that Czech Derain, that oddity of history, would be a disruption, an intrusive presence on the wall of that place. How could he ever have thought of taking it back with him? That painting doesn't belong there where he lives with his dear deceased. He'd never even mentioned it to her. That painting has nothing to do with her, with the two of them, with their life.

Then he thinks: if one little painting could disrupt his life with the dead woman, how much more disruptive would be the constant, unrelenting presence of a whole country, a country she never saw!

The sun dips toward the horizon; he is in the car on the road to Prague; the landscape slips away around him, the landscape of his small country whose people were willing to die for it, and he knows that there exists something even smaller, with an even stronger appeal to his compassionate love: he sees two easy chairs turned to face each other, the lamp and the flower bowl on the window ledge, and the slender fir tree his wife planted in front of the house, a fir tree that looks like an arm she'd raised from afar to show him the way back home.

39

When Skacel locked himself into the house of sadness for three hundred years, it was because he expected his country to be engulfed forever by the empire of the East. He was wrong. Everyone is wrong about the future. Man can only be certain about the present moment. But is that quite true either? Can he really know the present? Is he in a position to make any judgment about it? Certainly not. For how can a person with no knowledge of the future understand the meaning of the present? If we do not know what future the present is leading us toward, how can we say whether this present is good or bad, whether it deserves our concurrence, or our suspicion, or our hatred?

In 1921 Arnold Schoenberg declares that because of him German music will continue to dominate the world for the next hundred years. Twelve years later he is forced to leave Germany forever. After the war, in America, laden with honors, he is still convinced that his work will be celebrated forever. He faults Igor Stravinsky for paying too much attention to his contemporaries and disregarding the judgment of the future. He expects posterity to be his most reliable ally. In a scathing letter to Thomas Mann he looks to the period "after two or three hundred years," when it will finally become clear which of the two was the greater, Mann or he! Schoenberg dies in 1951. For the next two decades his work is hailed as the greatest of the century, venerated by the most brilliant of the young composers, who declare themselves his disciples; but thereafter it recedes from both concert halls and memory. Who plays it nowadays, at the turn of this century? Who looks to him? No, I don't mean to make foolish fun of his presumptuousness and say he overestimated himself. A thousand times no! Schoenberg did not overestimate himself. He overestimated the future.

Did he commit an error of thinking? No. His thinking was correct, but he was living in spheres that were too lofty. He was conversing with the greatest Germans, with Bach and Goethe and Brahms and Mahler, but, however intelligent they might be, conversations carried on in the higher stratospheres of the mind are always myopic about what goes on, with no reason or logic, down below: two great armies are battling to the death over sacred causes; but some minuscule plague bacterium comes along and lays them both low.

Schoenberg was aware that the bacterium existed. As early as 1930 he wrote: "Radio is an enemy, a ruthless enemy marching irresistibly forward, and any resistance is hopeless"; it "force-feeds us music . . . regardless of whether we want to hear it, or whether we can grasp it," with the result that music becomes just noise, a noise among other noises.

Radio was the tiny stream it all began with. Then came other technical means for reproducing, proliferating, amplifying sound, and the stream became an enormous river. If in the past people would listen to music out of love for music, nowadays it roars everywhere and all the time, "regardless whether we want to hear it," it roars from loudspeakers, in cars, in restaurants, in elevators, in the streets, in waiting rooms, in gyms, in the earpieces of Walkmans, music rewritten, reorchestrated, abridged, and stretched out, fragments of rock, of jazz, of opera, a flood of everything jumbled together so that we don't know who composed it (music become noise is anonymous), so that we can't tell beginning from end (music become noise has no form): sewage-water music in which music is dying.

Schoenberg saw the bacterium, he was aware of the danger, but deep inside he did not grant it much importance. As I said, he was living in the very lofty spheres of the mind, and pride kept him from taking seriously an enemy so small, so vulgar, so repugnant, so contemptible. The only great adversary worthy of him, the sublime rival whom he battled with verve and severity, was Igor Stravinsky. That was the music he charged at, sword flashing, to win the favor of the future.

But the future was a river, a flood of notes where composers' corpses drifted among the fallen leaves and torn-away branches. One day Schoenberg's dead body, bobbing about in the raging waves, collided with Stravinsky's, and in a shamefaced late-day reconciliation the two of them journeyed on together toward nothingness (toward the nothingness of music that is absolute din).

40

To recall: when Irena stopped with her husband on the embankment of the river running through a French provincial town, she had seen felled trees on the far bank and at the same moment was hit by a sudden volley of music loosed from a loudspeaker. She had clapped her hands over her ears and burst into tears. A few months later she was at home with her dying husband. From the next apartment music thundered. Twice she rang the doorbell and begged the neighbors to turn off the sound system, and twice in vain. Finally she shouted: "Stop that hideous racket! My husband is dying! Do you hear? Dying! Dying!"

During her first few years in France, she used to listen a lot to the radio, for it acquainted her with French language and life, but after Martin died, because of the music she had come to dislike, she no longer took pleasure in it; the news did not follow in sequence as it used to, instead the reports were set apart by three seconds, or eight or fifteen seconds, of that music, and year by year those little interludes swelled insidiously. She thereby grew intimately acquainted with what Schoenberg called "music become noise."

She is lying on the bed alongside Gustaf; overexcited at the prospect of her rendezvous, she fears for her sleep; she already swallowed one sleeping tablet, she drowsed off and, waking in the middle of the night, she took another two, then out of despair, out of nervousness, she turned on a little radio beside her pillow. To get back to sleep she wants to hear a human voice, some talk that will seize her thoughts, carry her off to another place, calm her down, and put her to sleep; she switches from station to station, but only music pours out from everywhere, sewage-water music, fragments of rock, of jazz, of opera, and it's a world where she can't talk to anybody because everybody's singing and yelling, a world where nobody talks to her because everybody's prancing around and dancing.

On the one side the sewage-water music, on the other a snore, and Irena, besieged, yearns for open space around her, a space to breathe, but she stumbles over the pale inert body that fate has dropped into her path like a sack of sludge. She is gripped by a fresh surge of hatred for Gustaf, not because his body is neglecting hers (Ah, no! she could never make love with him again!) but because his snores are keeping her awake and she's in danger of ruining the encounter of her life, the encounter that is to take place soon, in about eight hours, for morning is coming on, but sleep is not, and she knows she's going to be tired, edgy, her face made ugly and old.

Finally the intensity of her hatred acts as a narcotic, and she falls asleep. When she wakes, Gustaf has already gone out, while the little radio by her pillow is still emitting the music become noise. She has a headache and feels worn out. She would willingly stay in bed, but Milada said she would be coming by at ten o'clock. But why is she coming today? Irena hasn't the slightest desire to be with anyone at all!

41

Built on a slope, the house showed just one of its stories at street level. When the door opened Josef was assailed by the amorous onslaught of a huge German shepherd. Only after a while did he catch sight of N., laughing as he quieted the dog and led Josef along a hallway and down a long stairway to a two-room garden apartment where he lived with his wife; she was there, friendly, and she offered her hand.

"Upstairs," N. said, pointing to the ceiling, "the apartments are much roomier. My daughter and son live there with their families. The villa belongs to my son. He's a lawyer. Too bad he's not home. Listen," he said, dropping his voice, "if you want to come back here to live, he'll help you, he'll take care of things for you."

These words reminded Josef of the day forty

years earlier when, in that same voice lowered to indicate secrecy, N. had offered his friendship and his help.

"I told them about you," N. went on, and he shouted toward the stairwell several names that must have belonged to his progeny; when Josef saw all those grandchildren and great-grandchildren coming down the stairs, he had no idea whose they were. Anyhow, they were all beautiful, stylish (Josef couldn't tear his eyes off a blond, the girlfriend of one of the grandsons, a German girl who spoke not a word of Czech), and all of them, even the girls, looked taller than N.; among them he was like a rabbit caught in a tangle of weeds visibly springing up around and above him.

Like fashion models strutting a runway, they smiled wordlessly until N. asked them to leave him alone with his friend. His wife stayed indoors, and the two men went out into the garden.

The dog followed them, and N. remarked: "I've never seen him so excited by a visitor. It's as if he knows what you do for a living." Then he showed Josef some fruit trees and described his labors laying out the grassy plots set off by narrow pathways, so that for some time the conversation stayed distant from the subjects Josef had vowed to raise; finally he managed to interrupt his friend's botanical lecture and ask him about his life during the twenty years they had not seen each other.

"Let's not talk about it," said N., and in answer to Josef's inquiring look, he laid an index finger on his heart. Josef did not understand the meaning of the gesture: was it that the political events had affected him so profoundly, "to the heart?" or had he gone through a serious love affair? or had a heart attack?

"Someday I'll tell you about it," he added, turning aside any discussion.

The conversation was not easy; whenever Josef stopped walking to shape a question better, the dog took it as permission to jump up and set his paws on Josef's belly.

"I remember what you always used to say," N. remarked. "That a person becomes a doctor because he's interested in diseases; he becomes a veterinarian out of love for animals."

"Did I really say that?" Josef asked, amazed. He remembered that two days earlier he had told his sister-in-law that he'd chosen his profession as a rebellion against his family. So had he acted out of love, and not rebellion? In a single vague cloud he saw filing past him all the sick animals he had known; then he saw his veterinary clinic at the back of his brick house, where tomorrow (yes, in exactly twenty-four hours!) he would open the door to greet the day's first patient; a slow smile spread across his face.

He had to force himself back to the conversation barely begun: he asked whether N. had been attacked for his political past; N. said no; according to him, people knew he had always helped those the regime was giving trouble. "I don't doubt it," Josef said (he really didn't), but he pressed on: how did N. himself see his whole past life? As a mistake? As a defeat? N. shook his head, saying that it was neither the one nor the other. And finally Josef asked what N. thought of the very swift, harsh reestablishment of capitalism. Shrugging, N. replied that under the circumstances there was no other solution.

No, the conversation never managed to get going. Josef thought at first that N. found his questions indiscreet. Then he corrected himself: not so much indiscreet as outdated. If his sister-in-law's vindictive dream should come true and N. were indicted and tried in court, maybe he would reassess his Communist past to explain and defend it. But in the absence of any such trial, that past was remote from him these days. He didn't live there anymore.

Josef recalled a very old idea of his, which at the time he had considered to be blasphemous: that adherence to Communism has nothing to do with Marx and his theories; it was simply that the period gave people a way to fulfill the most diverse psychological needs: the need to look nonconformist; or the need to obey; or the need to punish the wicked; or the need to be useful; or the need to march forward into the future with youth; or the need to have a big family around you.

In good spirits, the dog barked and Josef said to himself: the reason people are quitting Communism today is not that their thinking has changed or undergone a shock, but that Communism no longer provides a way to look nonconformist or obey or punish the wicked or be useful or march forward with youth or have a big family around you. The Communist creed no longer answers any need. It has become so unusable that everyone drops it easily, never even noticing.

Still, the original goal of his visit was unfulfilled: to make it clear to N. that in some imaginary courtroom he, Josef, would defend him. To achieve this he would first show N. that he was not blindly enthusiastic about the world that had sprung up here since Communism, and he described the big advertisement on the square back in his hometown, in which an incomprehensible acronym-agency proposes its services to the Czechs by showing them a white hand and a black hand clasped together: "Tell me," he said. "Is this still our country?"

He expected to hear a sarcastic response about worldwide capitalism homogenizing the planet, but N. was silent. Josef went on: "The Soviet empire collapsed because it could no longer hold down the nations that wanted their independence. But those nations—they're less independent than ever now. They can't choose their own economy or their own foreign policy or even their own advertising slogans."

"National independence has been an illusion for a long time now," said N.

"But if a country is not independent and doesn't even want to be, will anyone still be willing to die for it?"

"Being willing to die isn't what I want for my children."

"I'll put it another way: does anyone still love this country?"

N. slowed his steps: "Josef," he said, touched. "How could you ever have emigrated? You're a patriot!" Then, very seriously: "Dying for your country—that's all finished. Maybe for you time stopped during your emigration. But they—they don't think like you anymore."

"Who?"

N. tipped his head toward the upper floors of the house, as if to indicate his brood. "They're somewhere else."

42

During these remarks the two friends came to a halt; the dog took advantage of it: he reared up and set his paws on Josef, who petted him. N. contemplated this man-dog couple for a time, increasingly touched. As if he were only just now taking full account of the twenty years they hadn't seen each other: "Ah, I'm so happy you came!"

He tapped Josef on the shoulder and drew him over to sit beneath an apple tree. And at once Josef knew: the serious, important conversation he had come for would not take place. And to his surprise, that was a comfort, it was a liberation! After all, he hadn't come here to put his friend through an interrogation!

As if a lock had clicked open, their conversation took off, freely and agreeably, a chat between two old pals: a few scattered memories, news of mutual friends, funny comments, and paradoxes and jokes. It was as if a gentle, warm, powerful breeze had taken him up in its arms. Josef felt an irrepressible joy in talking. Ah, such an unexpected joy! For twenty years he had barely spoken Czech. Conversation with his wife was easy, Danish having turned into a private jargon for themselves. But with other people he was always conscious of choosing his words, constructing a sentence, watching his accent. It seemed to him that when Danes talked they were running nimbly, while he was trudging along behind, lugging a twenty-kilo load. Now, though, the words leaped from his mouth on their own, without his having to hunt for them, monitor them. Czech was no longer the unknown language with the nasal timbre that had startled him at the hotel in his hometown. He recognized it now, and he savored it. Using it, he felt light, like after a diet. Talking was like flying, and for the first time in his visit he was happy in his homeland and felt that it was his.

Stimulated by the pleasure beaming from his friend, N. grew more and more relaxed; with a complicitous grin he mentioned his long-ago secret mistress and thanked Josef for having once served as an alibi for him with his wife. Josef did not recall the episode and was sure N. was confusing him with someone else. But the alibi story, which took N. a long time to tell, was so fine, so funny, that Josef ended up acquiescing in his supposed role as protagonist. He sat with his head tilted back, and through the leaves the sun lighted a beatific smile on his face.

It was in this state of well-being that N.'s wife surprised them: "You'll have lunch with us?"

He looked at his watch and stood up. "I've got an appointment in half an hour!"

"Then come back tonight! We'll have dinner together," N. urged warmly.

"Tonight I'll already be back home!"

"By 'back home' you mean—"

"In Denmark."

"It's so strange to hear you say that. So then this isn't home to you anymore?" asked N.'s wife.

"No. It's there."

There was a long silence and Josef expected questions: If Denmark really is your home, what's your life like there? And with whom? Tell about it! Tell us! Describe your house! Who's your wife? Are you happy? Tell us! Tell us!

But neither N. nor his wife asked any such question. For a moment, a low wooden fence and a fir tree flickered across Josef's mind.

"I must go," he said, and they all moved toward the stairs. As they climbed, they were quiet, and in that silence Josef was suddenly struck by his wife's absence; there was not a trace of her here. In the three days he'd spent in this country, no one had said a single word about her. He understood: if he stayed here, he would lose her. If he stayed here, she would vanish.

They stopped on the sidewalk outside, shook hands once again, and the dog leaned his paws on Josef's belly.

Then the three of them watched Josef move away until he vanished from their sight.

43

When after so many years she saw Irena at the restaurant among other women, Milada was overcome by tenderness for her; one detail in particular enchanted her: Irena recited a verse by Jan Skacel. In the little land of Bohemia, it is an easy thing to meet and approach a poet. Milada had known Skacel, a thickset man with a hard face that looked chipped out of rock, and she had adored him with the naiveté of a very young girl from another time. Now his collected poems have just been published in a single volume, and Milada has brought it as a gift to her friend.

Irena leafs through the book: "Do people still read poetry these days?"

"Hardly at all," says Milada, and then she recites a few lines by heart: " *'At noon, sometimes, you can see the night moving off toward the river. . . .'* Or listen to this: *'. . . ponds, water laid flat on its back.'* Or—there are some evenings, Skacel says, when the air is so soft and fragile that *'you can walk barefoot on broken glass.'* "

Listening to her, Irena remembers sudden

160

apparitions that used to spring without warning into her head during the early years of her emigration. They were fragments of that very landscape.

"Or this image: '... *on horseback, death and a peacock...*'" Milada recited the words in a voice that trembled faintly: they always called up this vision: a horse moving across fields; on its back a skeleton with a scythe in hand, and behind, riding pillion, a peacock with tail unfurled, splendid and shimmering like vanity eternal.

Irena gazes gratefully at Milada, the one friend she has found in this country; she gazes at her round pretty face made rounder yet by her hairstyle; because Milada is silent now, lost in thought, her wrinkles have vanished in the immobility of her skin and she looks like a young woman; Irena hopes she will not speak, not recite poetry, will stay motionless and beautiful for a long while.

"You've always worn your hair that way, haven't you? I've never seen you with any other hairstyle."

As if to sidestep the topic, Milada said: "So, are you finally going to make a decision someday?"

"You know very well that Gustaf has offices in Prague and Paris both!"

"But as I understand it, Prague is where he'd like to live."

"Listen, commuting back and forth between Paris and Prague is fine with me. I have my work in both places, Gustaf is my only boss, we manage, we improvise."

"What is it that holds you in Paris? Your daughters?"

"No. I don't want to cling to their lives."

"Have you got somebody there?"

"Nobody." Then: "My own apartment." Then: "My independence." And again, slowly: "I've always had the sense that my life is run by other people. Except for a few years after Martin died. Those were the toughest years, I was alone with my children, I had to cope by myself. Complete poverty. You won't believe this, but nowadays when I look back, those are my happiest years."

She is shocked, herself, at having called "happiest" the years after her husband's death, and she corrects herself: "What I mean is, that was the one time I was master of my own life."

162

She stops. Milada does not break the silence, and Irena goes on: "I married very young, solely to escape from my mother. But for just that reason, it was a decision that was forced, not really free. And on top of it, to escape my mother I married a man who was an old friend of hers. Because the only people I knew were her crowd. So even married, I was still under her watchful eye."

"How old were you?"

"Just turned twenty. And from then on, everything was determined once and for all. I made one mistake then, a mistake that's hard to define and impossible to grasp, but one that determined my entire life and that I never managed to repair."

"An irreparable mistake committed at the age of ignorance."

"Yes."

"That's the age people marry, have their first child, choose a profession. Eventually we come to know and understand a lot of things, but it's too late, because a whole life has already been determined at a stage when we didn't know a thing."

"Yes, yes!" Irena agrees, "even my emigration! That was also just the consequence of my earlier decisions. I emigrated because the secret police wouldn't leave Martin alone. He couldn't go on living here. But I could have. I stood by my husband, and I don't regret it. But still, my emigrating wasn't my own doing, my decision, my freedom, my fate. My mother pushed me toward Martin, and Martin took me abroad."

"Yes, I remember. The decision was made without you."

"Even my mother didn't object."

"Quite the contrary, it suited her fine."

"What do you mean? The house?"

"Everything's a matter of property."

"You're turning back into a Marxist," says Irena with a slight smile.

"Have you noticed how after forty years of Communism, the bourgeoisie landed on its feet again in just a few days? They survived in a thousand ways—some of them jailed, some thrown out of their jobs, others who even did very nicely, had brilliant careers, ambassadors, professors. Now their sons and grandsons are back together again, a kind of secret fraternity, they've taken over the banks, the newspapers, the parliament, the government."

"You really still are a Communist."

"The word doesn't mean a thing anymore. But it's true I am still a girl from a poor family."

She pauses, and various images go through her head: a girl from a poor family in love with a boy from a rich family; a young woman looking to Communism to find meaning for her life; after 1968 a mature woman who embraces the dissident movement and suddenly discovers a world far broader than before: not only Communists turning against the Party, but also priests and former political prisoners and downgraded members of the high bourgeoisie. And then after 1989, as if waking from a dream, she turns back into what she was when she started: an aging girl from a poor family.

"Don't be offended at my asking," says Irena, "you've told me before, but I forget: where were you born?"

Milada names a small city.

"I'm having lunch today with someone from there."

"Who's that?"

Hearing his name, Milada smiles: "I see he's still jinxing me. I was hoping to take you to lunch myself. Too bad."

44

He arrived on time but she was already waiting for him in the hotel lobby. He led her into the dining room and sat her down across from him at the table he had reserved.

After some talk, she breaks in: "Well, how do you like it here? Would you stay on?"

"No," he says; then in turn he asks: "What about you? What's holding you here?"

"Nothing."

The response is so trenchant and so like his own that they both burst into laughter. Their agreement is sealed thereby, and they set to talking with gusto, with gaiety.

He orders the meal, and when the waiter hands him the wine list Irena takes it herself: "You do the meal, I'll do the wine!" She sees some French wines on the list and selects one of those: "Wine is a matter of honor with me. They don't know a thing about wine, our countrymen, and you, dulled by your barbaric Scandinavia, you know even less."

She tells him how her friends refused to drink

the Bordeaux she provided them: "Imagine, a 1985 vintage! and to make a point, to teach me a lesson in patriotism, they drank beer! Later on they felt sorry for me, they were already drunk on the beer and they kept on drinking, with the wine!"

She tells the story, she's funny, they laugh.

"The worst thing is, they kept talking to me about things and people I knew nothing about. They refused to see that after all this time, their world has evaporated from my head. They thought with all my memory blanks I was trying to make myself interesting. To stand out. It was a very strange conversation: I'd forgotten who they had been; they weren't interested in who I'd become. Can you believe that not one person here has ever asked me a single question about my life abroad? Not one single question! Never! I keep having the sense that they want to amputate twenty years of my life from me. Really, it does feel like an amputation. I feel shortened, diminished, like a dwarf."

He likes her, and he likes her story, too. He understands her, he agrees with everything she's saying.

"And what about in France?" he says. "Do your friends there ask you any questions?"

She is about to say yes, but then she thinks again; she wants to be precise, and she speaks slowly: "No, of course not! But when people spend a lot of time together, they assume they know each other. They don't ask themselves any questions and they don't worry about it. They're not interested in each other, but it's completely innocent. They don't realize it."

"That's true. It's only when you come back to the country after a long absence that you notice the obvious: people aren't interested in one another, it's normal."

"Yes, it's normal."

"But I had something else in mind. Not about you, or about your life—not you as a person. I was thinking about your experience. About what you'd seen, what had happened to you. Your French friends couldn't have any conception of that."

"Oh, the French, you know—they have no need for experience. With them, judgments precede experience. When we got there, they didn't need any information from us. They were already

168

thoroughly informed that Stalinism is an evil and emigration is a tragedy. They weren't interested in what we thought, they were interested in us as living proof of what they thought. So they were generous to us and proud of it. When Communism collapsed all of a sudden, they looked hard at me, an investigator's look. And after that something soured. I didn't behave the way they expected."

She drinks a little wine; then: "They had really done a lot for me. They saw me as the embodiment of an émigré's suffering. Then the time came for me to confirm that suffering by my joyous return to the homeland. And that confirmation didn't happen. They felt duped. And so did I, because up till then I'd thought they loved me not for my suffering but for my self."

She tells him about Sylvie. "She was disappointed that I didn't rush home the first day to man the barricades in Prague!"

"What barricades?"

"Of course there were none, but Sylvie imagined there were. I wasn't able to come to Prague until a few months later, after the fact, and I did stay for a while then. When I got back to Paris, I had a terrific need to talk to her, you know, I really loved her, and I wanted to tell her all about it, discuss it all, the shock of going back to your country after twenty years, but she wasn't so eager to see me anymore."

"Did you quarrel?"

"Oh no. Just, I wasn't an émigré anymore. I wasn't interesting anymore. So, gradually, amicably, with a smile, she stopped calling."

"So who've you got to talk with? Who thinks the way you do?"

"No one." Then: "You."

45

They fell silent. And she repeated, her tone almost grave: "You." And she added: "Not here. In France. Better yet, somewhere else. Anywhere."

With these words, she offered him her future. And although Josef has no interest in the future, he feels happy with this woman who so visibly desires him. As if he were way back in the past, back in the years he used to go picking up girls in Prague. As if those years were inviting him now to take up the thread where he broke it off. He feels young again in the company of this stranger, and suddenly it seems unacceptable to cut short the afternoon for an appointment with his step-daughter.

"Will you excuse me? I have to make a phone call." He gets up and walks toward a booth.

She watches his slightly stooped figure as he lifts the receiver; from that distance she sees his age more clearly. At the Paris airport he had looked younger; now she sees that he must be fif-teen or twenty years older than she; like Martin, like Gustaf. That doesn't dishearten her; on the contrary it gives her the reassuring sense that however daring and risky it may be, this adven-ture fits the pattern of her life and is less mad than it seems (I note: she feels encouraged the way Gustaf did, years back, when he learned Martin's age).

He has barely given his name on the phone when the stepdaughter attacks him: "You're call-ing to say you're not coming."

"That's right. After all these years, I have so many things to do. I don't have a minute to spare. Do excuse me."

"You leave when?"

He is about to say, "Tonight," but it occurs to him that she might try to find him at the airport. He lies: "Tomorrow morning."

"And you have no time to see me? Even between two other appointments? Even late tonight? I can get free whenever you say!"

"No."

"I'm your wife's daughter, after all!"

The emphatic way she nearly shouts that last line reminds him of everything that used to drive him wild in this country. He hardens his stance and looks for a biting retort.

She beats him to it: "You're not talking! You don't know what to say! Just so you know, Mama warned me not to call you. She told me what an egotist you are! What a filthy little egotist!"

She hangs up.

Walking back to the table, he feels spattered with filth. Suddenly, illogically, a thought crosses his mind: I've had a lot of women in this country but no sister. He is startled by the line and by the word "sister"; he slows his step to breathe in that peaceful word: "sister." It's true, in this country he had never found any sister.

"Something unpleasant happen?"

"Nothing important," he replied as he sat down. "But unpleasant, yes."

He is quiet.

She too. Her fatigue reminds her of the sedatives from her sleepless night. Hoping to fight it off, she pours the last of the wine into her glass and drinks it. Then she lays her hand on his: "We're not happy here. Let me buy you a drink."

They move into the bar, where music is playing, loud.

She recoils, then gets hold of herself: she does want some alcohol. At the counter they each drink a glass of cognac.

He looks at her: "What's the matter?"

She nods toward the speakers.

"The music? Let's go to my room."

46

Learning of his presence in Prague through Irena was quite a remarkable coincidence. But by a certain age, coincidences lose their magic, no longer surprise, become run-of-the-mill. The memory of

Josef does not disturb her. With bitter humor she merely recalls that he used to enjoy scaring her with the threat of loneliness and that here he had just condemned her to eating her midday meal alone.

The way he talked about loneliness. Perhaps the reason the word lingers in her memory is because at the time it seemed so incomprehensible: as a girl with two brothers and two sisters, she detested crowds; for studying, or reading, she had no room of her own and had a hard time finding even a corner to withdraw to. Clearly they had different concerns, but she understood that in her boyfriend's mouth the word "loneliness" took on a more abstract, a grander meaning: going though life without drawing anyone's interest; talking without being heard; suffering without stirring compassion; thus, living as she has in fact lived ever since then.

In a neighborhood far from her house, she's parked her car and starts looking for a bistro. When she has no one to lunch with, she never goes to a restaurant (where, on an empty chair across the table, loneliness would sit down and watch her), but instead eats a sandwich at a counter. Passing a shopwindow, she catches a glimpse of her own reflection. She stops. Looking at herself is her vice, perhaps the only one. Pretending to look over the merchandise, she takes a look at herself: the brown hair, the blue eyes, the round outline of the face. She knows she is beautiful, has always known it, and it is her sole good fortune.

Then she realizes that what she is seeing is not only her vaguely reflected face but the window display of a butcher shop: a hanging carcass, severed haunches, a pig's head with a friendly, touching muzzle, and, farther into the shop, the plucked bodies of poultry with their claws lifted, impotently and humanly lifted, and suddenly horror shoots through her, her face crumples, she clenches her fists and strains to banish the nightmare.

Today Irena asked her the question she hears from time to time: why she has never changed her hairstyle. No, she never has changed it and she never will change it because she is beautiful only if she keeps wearing her hair the way it is arranged around her head now. Knowing the chatty indiscretion of hairdressers, she found herself one in a suburb where there wasn't a chance any of her friends would come wandering through. She had to guard the secret of her left ear at the cost of enormous discipline and an elaborate system of precautions. How was she to reconcile men's desire with the desire to be beautiful in their eyes? At first she had tried for a compromise (desperate journeys abroad, where nobody knew her and no indiscretion could betray her); then, later on, she had gone radical and sacrificed her erotic life to her beauty.

Standing at a bar, she slowly sips a beer and eats a cheese sandwich. She does not hurry; there is nothing she must do. All her Sundays are like that: in the afternoon she'll read, and at night she'll have a lonely meal at home.

47

Irena felt the fatigue still dogging her. Alone in the room for a few minutes, she opened the minibar and took out three tiny bottles of various liquors. She opened one and drank it down. She slipped the other two into her purse, which she laid on the night table. There she noticed a book in Danish: *The Odyssey*.

"I thought about Odysseus too," she tells Josef when he returns.

"He was away from his country like you. For twenty years."

"Twenty years?"

"Yes, twenty years exactly."

"But at least he was pleased to be back."

"That's not certain. He saw that his countrymen had betrayed him, and he killed a lot of them. I don't think he can have been much loved."

"Penelope loved him, though."

"Maybe."

"You're not sure?"

"I've read and reread the passage on their reunion. At first she didn't recognize him. Then, when things were already clear to everyone else, when the suitors were killed and the traitors punished, she put him through new tests to be sure it really was he. Or rather to delay the moment when they would be back in bed together."

"That's understandable, don't you think? A

person must be paralyzed after twenty years. Was she faithful to him all that time?"

"She couldn't help but be. All eyes on her. Twenty years of chastity. Their night of lovemaking must have been difficult. I imagine that over those twenty years, Penelope's organs would have tightened, shrunk."

"She was like me!"

"What?"

"No, don't worry!" she exclaims, laughing. "I'm not talking about mine! They haven't shrunk!"

And, suddenly giddy with the explicit mention of her sex organs, her voice lower, she slowly repeats the last sentence translated into dirty words. And then yet again, in a voice lower yet, in words yet more obscene.

How unexpected! How intoxicating! For the first time in twenty years, he hears those dirty Czech words and instantly he is aroused to a degree he has never been since he left this country, because all those words—coarse, dirty, obscene—only have power over him in his native language (in the language of Ithaca), since it is through that language, through its deep roots, that the arousal of generations and generations surges up in him. Until this moment these two have not even kissed. And now thrillingly, magnificently aroused, in a matter of seconds they begin to make love.

Their accord is total, for she too is aroused by the words she has neither said nor heard for so many years. A total accord in an explosion of obscenities! Ah, how impoverished her life has been! All the vices missed out on, all the infidelities left unrealized—all of that she is avid to experience. She wants to experience everything she ever imagined and never experienced, voyeurism, exhibitionism, the indecent presence of other people, verbal enormities; everything she can now do she tries to do, and what cannot be done she imagines with him aloud.

Their accord is total, for deep down Josef knows (and he may even want it so) that this erotic session is his last; he too is making love as if he hopes to sum up everything, his past adventures and those that will no longer happen. For each of them it is a tour through sexual life at high speed: the daring moves that lovers come to only after many encounters, if not many years, they accomplish in a rush, the one stimulating the other, as if they hope to compress into one single afternoon everything they have missed and are going to miss.

Then, winded, they lie side by side on their backs, and she says: "Ah, it's years since I've made love! You won't believe me, it's years since I've made love!"

That sincerity moves him, strangely, deeply; he shuts his eyes. She takes advantage of the moment to lean over to her purse and slip a tiny bottle out of it; swiftly, discreetly, she drinks.

He opens his eyes: "Don't drink, don't! You'll be drunk!"

"Leave me alone!" she defends herself. Feeling the fatigue that won't be driven off, she'll do whatever it takes to hold onto her fully wakened senses. That is why, even though he's watching, she empties the third little bottle and then as if to explain herself, as if to excuse herself, she repeats that she hasn't made love for a long while, and this time she says it in dirty words from her native Ithaca and again the magic of the obscenity arouses Josef and he begins again to make love to her.

In Irena's head the alcohol plays a double role: it frees her fantasy, encourages her boldness, makes her sensual, and at the same time it dims her memory. She makes love wildly, lasciviously, and at the same time the curtain of oblivion wraps her lewdnesses in an all-concealing darkness. As if a poet were writing his greatest poem with ink that instantly disappears.

48

The mother set the disk into a big player and pressed several buttons to program the pieces she liked, then she plunged into the bathtub, and, with the door left open, she listened to the music. It was her personal selection of four dance pieces, a tango, a waltz, a Charleston, a rock-and-roll, which through the machine's technical prowess played over and over endlessly with no further intervention. She stood up in the tub, washed at length, stepped out, toweled herself down, slipped on her robe, and walked into the living room. Then Gustaf arrived after a long lunch with some Swedes passing through Prague, and he asked her where Irena was. She answered (mixing bad English with some Czech, simplified for his sake): "She phoned. She won't be back till late tonight. How was lunch?"

"Much too much!"

"Have a digestive," and she poured some liqueur into two glasses.

"That's something I never turn down!" Gustaf exclaimed, and he drank.

The mother whistled the tune of the waltz and undulated her hips; then, without a word, she laid her hands on Gustaf's shoulders and did a few dance steps with him.

"You're in a magnificent mood!" said Gustaf.

"Yes," the mother answered, and she went on dancing, her movements so overdrawn, so theatrical, that with short awkward bursts of laughter Gustaf executed some exaggerated steps and gestures himself. He went along with this parodical performance both to prove that he didn't want to spoil the fun and to recall, with bashful vanity, that he used to be an excellent dancer and still was. As they danced, the mother led him toward the great mirror on the wall, and the two of them turned their heads to watch themselves.

Then she let go of him and, without touching, they improvised routines facing the mirror; Gustaf was making dancing gestures with his hands and, like her, never took his eyes off their reflection. So he saw the mother's hand come to settle on his crotch.

The scene taking place illustrates an immemorial error of men: having appropriated for themselves the role of seducers, they never even consider any women but the ones they might desire; the idea doesn't occur to them that a woman who is ugly or old, or who simply stands outside their own erotic imaginings, might want to possess them. Sleeping with Irena's mother was to Gustaf so thoroughly unthinkable, fantastical, unreal that, struck dumb by her touch, he has no idea what to do: his first reflex is to lift her hand away; yet he does not dare; a commandment is graven in him since his childhood: thou shalt not be crude with a woman; so he goes on making his dancing motions and staring in stupefaction at the hand placed between his legs.

Her hand still on his crotch, the mother rocks in

place and keeps watching herself in the mirror; then she lets her robe gape open and Gustaf glimpses her opulent breasts and the dark triangle below; embarrassed, he feels his member swelling.

Without taking her eyes from the mirror, the mother finally lifts her hand away, but only to slip it into his trousers and grasp the naked member in her fingers. It grows harder and, still continuing her dance movements and gazing at the mirror, she exclaims admiringly in her vibrant alto voice: "Oh, oh! Unbelievable! Unbelievable!"

49

As he is making love, from time to time Josef looks discreetly at his watch: two hours left, an hour and a half left; this afternoon of love is fascinating, he doesn't want to miss any part of it, not a move, not a word, but the end is drawing near, ineluctable, and he must watch the time running out.

She too is thinking about the waning time; her

lewdness is growing the more reckless and fevered, her talk leaps from one fantasy to another as she senses that it is already too late, that this delirium is about to end and that her future lies empty. She says another few dirty words, but she says them in tears because, racked with sobs, she can't go on, she ceases all movement and pushes him away from her body.

They are lying side by side, and she says: "Don't go today, stay awhile."

"I can't."

She is still for a long time, then: "When will I see you again?"

He does not answer.

With sudden determination, she leaves the bed; she is not crying now; on foot facing him, she says without sentiment, abruptly aggressive: "Kiss me!"

He lies still, uncertain.

Motionless, she waits, staring at him with the whole weight of a life that has no future to it.

Unable to stand up to her gaze, he capitulates: he rises, approaches, sets his lips on hers.

She tastes his kiss, gauges the degree of his coldness, and says: "You're a bad man!"

Then she turns to her purse where it lies on the

night table. She pulls out a small ashtray and shows it to him. "Do you recognize this?"

He takes the ashtray and looks at it.

"Do you recognize it?" she repeats, harsh.

He does not know what to say.

"Look at the inscription!"

It is the name of a Prague bar. But that tells him nothing and he does not speak. She observes his discomfort with attentive, increasingly hostile mistrust.

He feels uneasy beneath her gaze, and just then, very briefly, there flickers the image of a window ledge with a bowl of flowers beside a lighted lamp. But the image vanishes, and again he sees the hostile eyes.

Now she understands everything: not only has he forgotten their meeting in the bar, but the truth is worse: he doesn't know who she is! he doesn't know her! in the airplane he did not know whom he was talking to. And suddenly she realizes: he has never addressed her by name!

"You don't know who I am!"

"What?" he says, sounding desperately awkward.

Like a prosecutor she says: "Then tell me my name!"

He is silent.

"What's my name? Tell me my name!"

"Names don't matter!"

"You've never called me by my name! You don't know me!"

"What?"

"Where did we meet? Who am I?"

He wants to calm her down, he takes her hand, she thrusts him away: "You don't know who I am! You picked up a strange woman! You made love with a stranger who offered herself to you! You took advantage of a misunderstanding! You used me like a whore! I was a whore to you, some unknown whore!"

She drops onto the bed and weeps.

He sees the three empty liquor vials scattered on the floor: "You've had too much to drink. It's stupid to drink so much!"

She isn't listening. Stretched flat on her belly, her body twitching spasmodically, all she can think of is the loneliness ahead.

Then, as if stricken with exhaustion, she stops crying and turns onto her back, unaware as her legs spread carelessly apart.

Josef is still standing at the foot of the bed; he

gazes at her crotch as if he were gazing into space, and suddenly he sees the brick house, with a fir tree. He looks at his watch. He can stay a half hour longer at the hotel. He has to get dressed and find a way to make her dress as well.

50

When he slid out of her body they were silent, and the only thing to be heard was the four pieces of music repeating endlessly. After a long while, in a distinct, almost solemn voice, as if she were reading out the clauses in a treaty, the mother said in her Czech-English: "We are strong, you and I. But we are good, too. We won't be harming anyone. Nobody will know a thing. You are free. You can whenever you want. But you're not obligated. With me you are free."

She said it this time without any hint of parody, in the most serious tone possible. And Gustaf, serious too, answers: "Yes, I understand."

"With me you are free," the words echo in him

for a long while. Freedom: he'd looked for that in her daughter but did not find it. Irena gave herself to him with all the weight of her life, whereas he wanted to live weightless. He was looking to her for an escape, and instead she loomed before him as a challenge; as a puzzle; as a feat to accomplish; as a judge to face.

He sees the body of his new mistress rise from the couch; she is standing, showing her body from the back, the powerful thighs padded with cellulite; that cellulite enchants him as if it expressed the vitality of an undulating, quivering, speaking, singing, jiggling, preening skin; when she bends to pick up her discarded robe from the floor, he cannot contain himself and, from where he lies naked on the couch, he strokes those magnificently rounded buttocks, he fingers that monumental, overabundant flesh whose generous prodigality comforts and calms him. A feeling of peace envelops him: for the first time in his life, sex is located away from all danger, away from conflict and drama, away from persecution, away from any accusation, away from worries; he has nothing to take care of, love is taking care of him, love as he's always wanted it and never had it:

189

love-repose; love-oblivion; love-desertion; love-carefreeness; love-meaninglessness.

The mother has gone into the bathroom, and he is alone: a few minutes ago he thought he had committed an enormous sin; but now he knows that his act of love had nothing to do with a vice, with a transgression or a perversion, that it was an utterly normal thing. It is with her, the mother, that he makes up a couple, a pleasantly ordinary, natural, suitable couple, a couple of serene old folks. From the bathroom comes the sound of water; he sits up on the couch and looks at his watch. In two hours he is expecting the son of his most recent mistress, a man, young, who admires him. Gustaf will introduce him this evening among his business friends. His whole life he's been surrounded by women! What a pleasure, finally, to have a son! He smiles and begins to look for his clothes where they're scattered on the floor.

He is already dressed when the mother returns from the bathroom, in a robe. The situation is very slightly solemn and thus embarrassing, as are all such situations when after the initial love-making, the lovers confront a future they are suddenly required to take on. The music is still playing, and at this delicate moment, as if it hoped to rescue them, it shifts from rock to tango. They obey the invitation, they come together and give over to that indolent monotone flood of sounds; they do not think; they let themselves be carried along and carried away; they dance, slowly and at length, with absolutely no parody.

51

Her sobs went on for a long time, and then, as if by a miracle, they stopped, followed by heavy breathing: she fell asleep; this change was startling and sadly laughable; she slept, profoundly and irretrievably. She had not changed position, she was still on her back with her legs spread.

He was still looking at her crotch, that tiny little area that, with admirable economy of space, provides for four sovereign functions: arousal, copulation, procreation, urination. He gazed a long while at that sad place with its spell broken, and was gripped by an immense, immense sadness.

He knelt by the bed, leaning over her gently snoring head; he felt close to this woman; he could imagine staying with her, being concerned with her; they had promised in the airplane not to inquire into each other's private life; he knew nothing about her, therefore, but one thing seemed clear: She was in love with him; prepared to go off with him, to give up everything, to begin everything over again. He knew she was calling on him for help. He had a chance, certainly his last, to be useful, to help someone, and among the multitude of strangers overpopulating the planet, to find a sister.

He began to dress, discreetly, silently, so as not to wake her.

52

As on every Sunday evening, she was alone in her modest impecunious-scientist studio apartment. She moved about the room and ate the same thing she had at noon: cheese, butter, bread, beer. A vegetarian, she is sentenced to such alimentary monotony. Since her stay at the mountain hospital, meat reminds her that her body could be cut up and eaten as easily as the body of a calf. Of course, people don't eat human flesh, it would terrify them. But that terror only confirms that a man can be eaten, masticated, swallowed, transmuted into excrement. And Milada knows that the terror of being eaten is only the effect of another more general terror that lies at the foundation of all of life: the terror of being a body, of existing in body form.

She finished her dinner and went into the bathroom to wash her hands. Then she looked up and saw herself in the mirror above the sink. This gaze was entirely different from the earlier one, when she was observing her beauty in a shopwindow. This time the look was tense; slowly she lifted the hair that framed her cheeks. She looked at herself, as if spellbound, for a long, a very long time; then she let the hair fall back into place, arranged it around her face, and returned to the room.

At the university she used to be seduced by the dreams of voyages to distant stars. What pleasure to escape far away into the universe, someplace where life expresses itself differently from here and needs no bodies! But despite all his amazing rockets, man will never progress very far in the universe. The brevity of his life makes the sky a dark lid against which he will forever crack his head, to fall back onto earth, where everything alive eats and can be eaten.

Misery and pride. "On horseback, death and a peacock." She was standing at the window, gazing at the sky. A starless sky, a dark lid.

53

He put all his belongings into the suitcase and glanced around the room so as not to leave anything behind. Then he sat down at the table, and on a hotel letterhead sheet he wrote:

"Sleep well. The room is yours till tomorrow at noon. . . ." He would have liked to say something very tender besides, but at the same time he was determined not to leave her a single false word. Finally, he added: ". . . my sister."

He laid the sheet on the rug beside the bed to make sure she would see it.

He picked up the DO NOT DISTURB card; as he left he turned to look again at her as she slept, and, in the corridor, he closed the door silently and hung the card on the knob.

In the lobby from all around him he heard Czech being spoken and again now it was flat and unpleasantly blasé, an unknown language.

Settling his bill, he said: "There's a woman still in my room. She will leave later." And to ensure that no one would give her an unpleasant look, he laid a five-hundred-korun note on the counter before the receptionist.

He climbed into a taxi and left for the airport. It was evening already. The plane took off toward a dark sky, then burrowed into clouds. After a few minutes the sky opened out, peaceful and friendly, strewn with stars. Through the porthole he saw, far off in the sky, a low wooden fence and a brick house with a slender fir tree like a lifted arm before it.